A BABY CHANGES EVERYTHING

A Hickory Ridge Novel

ISABELLE GRACE

ROSEWOOD
BOOKS

For my family and friends who continue to encourage, inspire and believe in me (you know who you are). This one's for you!

Published by Rosewood Books

ISBN (eBook): 978-1-83756-014-1
ISBN (Paperback): 978-1-83756-015-8
ISBN (Hardback): 978-1-83756-016-5

Previously published by the author as Drew's Hope.

PROLOGUE

Hope Logan had done some pretty stupid things over the years. Some flat-out embarrassing. Others indisputably more foolish and irresponsible. A few even perilously close to the danger zone. But in almost every instance, stupidity was the root cause with regret as the repercussion.

And if the man taking up a large portion of her bed was any indication, last night's total lapse in judgment was certainly no different.

What had she been thinking?

Of course, that question was the easiest to answer since it was clear she obviously hadn't been thinking at all. If she had, her head wouldn't be relentlessly pounding out a Patron-induced staccato against her skull, she wouldn't feel like something the cat dragged in, and more importantly, there wouldn't be a man sprawled in all his masculine glory on the other side of her bed.

And not just any man either. Because if her screwed-up life wasn't complicated enough, the man she'd slept with was none other than Drew Blackwood, one of the chief veterinarians on staff at Wakefield Equine Associates, where, as luck would have it, Hope was also employed. A place where she'd purposely and successfully kept her professional and personal lives separate.

Well, until last night anyway.

Jeesh Louise. If it wasn't bad enough she'd broken her own hard and fast rule to never get involved with someone she worked with, it was a million times worse when the person wasn't just another coworker but the lead vet on the team she was assigned. Ergo, her boss.

Only now, after last night's ill-fated turn of events, it also made him her lover. Or, at the very least, her one-night stand. Because not only was their sleeping together a colossal mistake in general, it would inevitably put a strain on their working relationship. Which was unfortunate, since they made one hell of a veterinary team.

But hey, with everything else in her life going to shit, why not ruin that too?

Oh well, not much she could do about it now.

Still, Hope lay motionless and pondered her options, hardly daring to breathe for fear of waking Drew. Since they'd ended up at her place, there was no way to make a quick getaway. But, maybe, if she carefully eased herself out of the bed and streaked straight to the bathroom, Drew would seize the opportunity to escape from what promised to be a terribly awkward morning after.

Mentally, Hope shook her head. That was purely wishful thinking on her part because if Drew had wanted to escape, he'd had ample opportunity to do so after they'd done the deed. But he didn't. Nope. Instead of bolting for the door when he had the chance, he'd stayed to tempt, tantalize, and quite effectively seduce her into rounds two, three, and four of mind-blowing, toe-curling sex before they both collapsed from sheer exhaustion.

And a few too many tequila shots.

As the morning sun streamed through the slats in the plantation blinds she hadn't given any thought to closing the night before, Hope grew increasingly more anxious. Things would definitely be uncomfortable when Drew finally awakened. How could they not when last night had been nothing more than the culmination of an emotionally charged day fueled significantly by a healthy dose of liquid courage?

God, she really was an idiot. In the span of one night, Hope had not only irrevocably jeopardized a successful working relationship, she'd likely also lost a damn good friend in the process.

Before she could berate herself further, Drew's eyes fluttered open. "Mornin'," he murmured, his voice thick and raspy with sleep. A slow smile eased into his whisker-stubbled cheeks as he reached out to pull her closer.

Yikes!

A shiver that had nothing to do with being cold zipped through Hope's entire body, reawakening every inch of flesh Drew had brought to life multiple times during the night. If her own physical reaction to his touch wasn't enough to contend with, the burgeoning effect of Drew's desire pressed rigidly against her hip.

Oh. My. Goodness.

For a hot second, Hope wished they could forget who they were for a little while longer. Keep the real world at bay while she lost herself in the infinite depths of his lake-blue eyes. Trail her fingers over the rippling cords of his hard-muscled physique while they rode the waves of passion to the height of paradise and beyond.

But that would be pure craziness, right? Last night Hope had wanted to escape. To block out the devastating news about her father and dull the excruciating pain in her heart. To lose herself in Drew's arms this morning would only serve to complicate matters between them more than they already were.

Right now, they both needed to man up and deal with the repercussions of their impulsive but oh-so-spectacular night together. Shifting, Hope disengaged herself from Drew's hold. She scooted to a sitting position, covered her nakedness with the canary yellow bed sheet, and sent up a prayer for strength.

And forgiveness.

Facing her, Drew propped himself on his elbow and narrowed his gaze. Even with his dark hair all sleep rumpled and the scruff of his beard shadowing his usually clean-shaven jaw, he still looked good enough to eat.

Damn him.

"Why do I get the feeling that if I'd woken up in my bed this morning, you wouldn't be in it?"

Hope hugged her knees to her chest. "Probably because I wouldn't." And that was the honest-to-God truth.

Sighing, Drew thrust his long, skilled fingers through his dark hair, disheveling it even more. "I was afraid of that."

Hope suppressed the urge to reach out. To assure him her compulsion to flee had nothing to do with him personally. That under entirely different circumstances, everything might be different. Like if they didn't work together. Or if he wasn't her supervisor.

Or if she hadn't been informed the day before that her father was dying.

For months, Hope had seen the subtle changes in Sam's health. She'd begged him to see the doctor, but he kept insisting he was just getting older and simply couldn't do things like he used to. Other times, he'd claim he was only fighting off a cold or the flu and he'd be fine in a day or two.

Yesterday, however, the doctor had informed them Sam wasn't going to be fine. He had stage four liver cancer, which had already spread through his lymphatic system. Although both chemo and radiation treatments were recommended, their purpose would be more palliative than curative.

When they'd returned to Sam's place, Hope had intended to stay with him but he'd insisted she go back to work. There was nothing she could do, and there wasn't any use bemoaning the hand fate had dealt him, Sam had assured her. He just needed a little time to absorb and process the news the doctor had given him.

Reluctantly, Hope went on to work, and within an hour of receiving the most devastating news of her life, she and Drew had answered a call for a mare in fetal distress. After three grueling hours of doing everything humanly possible to save the prematurely delivered foal as well as his mother, the colt had simply not been strong enough to survive.

That, combined with the earlier news from Sam's doctor, had hit Hope like an F5 tornado. She'd completely lost it. Like a dam bursting wide-open, uncontrollable sobs racked her entire body as tears flowed like rivers down her cheeks. At some point, Drew had pulled her into his arms, offering her comfort with his gentle caresses and soothing words.

His strength had been precisely what Hope had needed.

When she had no more tears left to cry, she'd uttered the words that would alter the course of their lives forever. "What do you say we go back to my place, order some pizza, and you can help me drown my sorrows in a bottle of tequila?"

Twelve hours later, here they were.

Yesterday had been one helluva day. Unfortunately, even after having the best sex of her life, today wasn't shaping up to be much better.

CHAPTER ONE

Twelve Weeks Later

Despite the awkwardness of the morning after their night together, Drew hadn't made as big a deal about them sleeping together as Hope feared he might. Although she suspected he may have wanted to explore the physical side of their relationship further, he'd understood when she'd expressed her concern about not wanting things to become weird between them or interfere with their work at the clinic.

By unspoken agreement, they'd tabled what had happened between them, both deciding it best to move forward with their lives as normally as possible. Especially while Hope dealt with her father's declining health and the repercussions of his prognosis.

In fact, if it hadn't been for Drew, Hope didn't know how she'd have survived the past couple of months. He'd been flexible with her schedule, offering his assistance as both a friend and coworker in whatever capacity she needed, and was never more than a phone call away.

When her father entered his final days, and in the two weeks since his passing, Drew had barely left her side. He'd been there when Sam had taken his final breath and had worked with Hospice to ensure all the appropriate calls and arrangements were made to have Sam's body transferred to the funeral home.

When she met with the minister to plan the service, he'd been with her, had coordinated with the staff at Wakefield to have their duties covered, and had answered calls and welcomed visitors who wished to offer condolences and make food for the repast, basically handling whatever needed doing.

On the day of the funeral, he drove Hope to the church, escorted her inside, and comforted her as she cried her heart out. When they returned to the fellowship hall after the interment, Drew remained by her side as she greeted those in attendance. It had heartened Hope to know that even though the only family she'd ever known was gone, she wasn't completely and utterly alone.

And after seeing the doctor this morning, Hope found out just how *un-alone* she truly was.

The appointment, scheduled a year in advance, was for her annual physical. Per usual, as Dr. Lawson conducted her exam, Hope answered the physician's routine questions regarding her general health and well-being. Yeah, she'd been a little more tired lately, but that was likely because her body no longer ran on nervous energy while she tried to juggle working full time, taking care of her father, and handling some of the farrier workload Sam had been too sick to do himself.

Any other symptoms?

Well, a few mornings, her stomach had been a bit queasy, but that was likely the result of her poor eating habits of late. Once she got up, put something in her belly, and started moving around, she was fine.

Except for this morning, when her stomach violently rejected the eggs and toast she'd eaten for breakfast. Probably because she was run down and had caught a touch of one of the many viruses going around, Hope rationalized to the doctor.

Or maybe they should run a few tests to be sure, Dr. Lawson suggested.

"You've been awfully quiet this morning. Is everything all right?" Drew asked as they restocked their supplies and equipment in the compartments built into the bed of his extended cab Ford F-350.

Hope wanted to laugh. Or cry. Bottom line, she doubted she would ever be *all right* again. Well, at least not for the foreseeable future anyway.

As if on cue, a wave of nausea swept through her stomach, crested, and rolled again. Hope leaned against the side of the truck, closed her eyes, and focused on breathing. In through her nose—*Please don't let me throw up.* Out through her mouth —*Not in front of Drew.* And repeat. *Please, please, please.*

No such luck. Instead of subsiding, the tempest brewing in her belly intensified until she was forced to give up the fight.

Pitching forward, Hope stretched outward to keep from puking all over her red-wing boots. For what seemed like an eternity, her body lurched as the contents of her stomach emptied onto the grass beside the parking lot of the clinic. When the retching waned into a mild case of dry heaves, she rested her hands on her jean-clad thighs but kept her body bent at the waist in case another round struck.

Beside her in an instant, Drew encircled her arm with his hand, steadying her. "You okay?" Concern encased each word.

Nodding, Hope sucked in one deep breath after another, praying for no reprise.

"What can I do?" Drew asked as he stroked his palm up and down her back.

Hope swiped the back of her hand against her mouth. "Can you get me some water, please?"

"Sure, but how about you sit down first." He led her over to the benches located in the back of the two-story stone and timber clinic built to resemble a stable. In a flash, he retrieved a water bottle from the stash they kept in the truck and, after removing the cap, handed it to Hope.

Hope took a sip and swished it around in her mouth before spitting it out. Then, she took a tentative swallow, praying it stayed in her stomach.

"What else can I do? Is there anything I can get you?"

Just a time machine to take us back about twelve weeks. Instead of voicing that thought, Hope shook her head. "No, I'm good. Thanks."

Crouching in front of her, Drew urged Hope to drink more of the water. She complied, taking a deep breath between each sip until her stomach no longer mimicked a volcano on the verge of eruption. When she looked up at Drew, Hope felt a tug in her chest at the concern reflected in his lake-blue eyes.

God, he had beautiful eyes.

"Is this why you went to the doctor this morning?"

Not intentionally. "No. It was just my annual checkup."

"Do you think it was something you ate?"

Oh, how Hope wished it were.

"Or maybe you have a virus. I heard something is going around." Reaching up, Drew laid the back of his fingers against her forehead. "Do you have a fever?"

Hope batted his hand away. "No. No fever." Sighing, she averted her gaze. "And it's not a virus or anything I ate either."

Dropping one denim-clad knee to the pavement, Drew crossed his wrists atop his opposite knee and leaned forward. "So, what do you think is wrong?"

Everything, Hope wanted to scream. But that wasn't accurate because there wasn't anything wrong. Unexpected, yes. And definitely one hell of a freaking surprise.

But considering she'd just tossed her cookies in front of him and likely would again, she might as well answer his question honestly. She forced herself to look him in the eye. "I'm pregnant." Not exactly the way she'd envisioned sharing the news of her pregnancy with the father of her baby, but then again, nothing in the past three months had been anything she expected.

Stunned, Drew was silent for a few beats as her words sank into his brain.

Hope.

Pregnant.

With his child.

Damn.

Drew eased onto the bench beside her. "How long have you known?"

"About three hours."

Three hours? Wow! "Is that why you went to the doctor?"

Hope shook her head. "No. Like I told you before, it was my annual physical."

"So, you didn't suspect you might be pregnant?" Though he was definitely more familiar with the estrous cycle of the equine species, Drew did have a basic grasp on how a woman's reproductive system functioned. And if he did the math correctly, he was fairly certain Hope should have gotten her period at least twice, if not three times, since they'd slept together twelve weeks ago.

She cut him with a slicing glare. "No. I didn't." Hope took another sip of water. "Maybe if I hadn't been trying to work a full-time job while also taking care of my terminally ill father, watching him die a slow, painful death, and then laying him to rest, I might have had a second to realize my monthly visitor had neglected to show up for three months in a row."

When she put it that way, Drew felt like a first-class ass.

"But fortunately, the doctor asked all the right questions this morning, which prompted her to run a few tests, and within an hour, she confirmed her suspicions. And to answer your next question, yes, I had every intention of telling you. I just needed to wrap my own head around the news first."

God, he was such a jerk. "I'm sorry, Hope." Sorry he had even considered Hope might have suspected she was pregnant before the doctor had mentioned the possibility. Sorry he'd asked the question out loud. Sorry he hadn't been more responsible that night. "I should have been better prepared. Done a better job of protecting you."

"You weren't alone that night, Drew. And as a willing participant, I had just as much responsibility to take precautions as you did."

Only neither of them had. Sure, it was easy enough to blame their carelessness solely on the Patron. Even give it considerable credit for lowering their inhibitions. But wanting Hope in the most intimate sense had absolutely nothing to do with the tequila. That was all him. And had been since the first day they met.

Now, because he'd been thinking—and feeling—with the wrong head three months ago, Hope was pregnant with his child. In the big scheme of things, the circumstances surrounding the conception didn't matter. What mattered now was what they were going to do as a result.

A million questions raced through his head. So many things for them to consider. So much for them to discuss and decide. He didn't have a clue where they should start. But there was one question that gnawed at him more than the rest. One he was reluctant to ask because he feared what Hope's answer might be. Yet one impossible to ignore.

"Are you going to have the baby?" Drew steeled himself against her response.

Hope looked at him like that was the absolute last question she expected from him. "Of course."

Relief washed over him like a cleansing rain. Okay, one obstacle down.

"But that doesn't mean I expect anything from you,

because I don't. I'm perfectly capable of handling everything on my own. Really."

Though he knew her words were meant to soothe, Drew found no comfort in them. "What about my expectations?" he countered, a sharpness he hadn't intended edging each word. "Because make no mistake, I do expect to be a part of our child's life." No matter what happened between them from this point forward, Drew wanted to be sure Hope understood that much from the jump.

Nodding, Hope swallowed visibly. "I didn't mean to upset you. I just didn't want you to feel obligated to go all 'do the right thing,' because I'm really okay with handling all this on my own."

Reaching out, Drew took her hand and threaded his fingers through hers. "But you don't have to handle everything by yourself, Hope." He squeezed her hand. "I want to be there for you. To help you and to share everything about this pregnancy with you."

"I'm sorry I let this happen, Drew. That I put us in this predicament. If I had just gone home by myself that night, none of this would have happened."

"Like you said, you weren't alone. I could have gone home anytime I wanted, but I didn't because I was exactly where I wanted to be. With you. I didn't have a single regret after the night we spent together, Hope." He squeezed her hand. "And I don't have any now either."

"How can you say that? Especially since you've barely had a minute to let everything sink in?"

"Because it's the truth." He leaned into her. "And because you're having my baby. That's all I need to know."

"But we're not ready to be parents." Sighing, she pulled her hand from his and covered her face with her palms. "At least, I'm not."

"I doubt anyone is ever totally ready."

"Yeah, well, I'm not even remotely ready." She dropped her hands to her thighs. "And I'm not sure I ever will be."

Panic suddenly clawed through him. "You said you were going to have the baby."

"I am. I'm just not sure about keeping it."

Her words hit him like a sucker punch straight to his gut. "You're thinking about giving the baby up for adoption?" She couldn't be serious, could she?

"It's an option to consider."

"Why?"

"Because I'm not ready to be a mother. I don't know what it takes. Besides, with my veterinary career just getting started, the timing couldn't be any worse."

"A lot of mothers have jobs outside the home, Hope. There's no reason why you can't as well."

"I know that."

For several minutes, they sat on the bench in silence, each deep in their own thoughts about the choices and challenges they faced in the coming months. Their potential differences in opinion. And the possible fallout that might ensue as a result.

Hope was right. They weren't ready to be parents, but the idea wasn't as daunting to him as it obviously was to her. Sure, in a perfect world, the circumstances of their impending parenthood would be much different. They would be in a committed relationship, most likely married. And they would have waited until they were ready to start a family before engaging in unprotected sex.

Only it wasn't a perfect world. Far from it, actually. If it were, Hope's father would have never been diagnosed with the cancer that eventually claimed his life. The mare would never have gone into premature labor. There would have been no pain Hope needed to numb with too many shots of tequila. And they never would have ended up in bed together.

Still, it was a night Drew would never forget. And until ten minutes ago, that had absolutely nothing to do with Hope being pregnant with his child.

No, what Drew remembered about that night—and despite his inebriated state, he did remember quite a bit—was that it had been the best night of his life. Not that he'd been intimate with scores of women in his thirty-four years, but there'd been enough for a fair comparison.

Quite frankly, no other woman had come close to the way Hope made him feel.

If anyone ever had, there was no way he'd still be dreaming about Hope three months later. Reliving their one night of unbridled passion. Waking up each morning with a raging hard-on. And wishing she were lying in his bed beside him so he could show her how desperately he wanted her.

But if wishes were horses, beggars would ride.

"So, what happens now?" Drew asked, not sure he was prepared to hear her answer but needing to know anyway.

With a slight shake of her head, Hope shrugged. "Guess I'll get fat, because I'll be eating for two, and we both know how much I like food. At some point, my feet will swell to the point where wearing shoes and boots will be damned near impossible. And from what I hear, I'll be riding quite the emotional rollercoaster, fueled by my very own jacked-up hormones."

Drew couldn't help but chuckle. At least Hope hadn't lost her sense of humor. "I was thinking more in terms of the baby. And us."

Hope exhaled slowly. "I don't know, Drew. I wish I did, but considering I had no idea there was a baby to consider until a few hours ago, I don't have the answers to give you right now."

"But it was enough time for you to consider giving the baby away?" He regretted the words as soon as they left his mouth.

Sort of.

"Considering doesn't mean doing. Do you have any idea

how many things have run through my mind since the doctor told me that I'm pregnant?"

"I have a pretty good idea," he countered. His mind hadn't stopped its own sprint yet.

"Then could we just have a minute to let everything sink in before we get balls deep in making decisions that will affect the rest of our lives?"

"As long as I'm a part of the decision-making process." He needed to make that point clear.

"I have no intention of excluding you. But right now, the only thing I can tell you for sure is that in about twenty-eight weeks, I'm going to give birth. Everything else, we can decide along the way."

"Together." He had to be sure.

"Yes. Together."

"That's all I ask." For now, anyway.

CHAPTER TWO

Two Weeks Later

"I'm sorry, Hope. I wish I had better news." Lucas Danforth rounded his massive mahogany desk and sat down in the tufted oxblood leather chair beside her. "Your daddy was one hell of a horseman, but he was a piss-poor manager of his finances."

And the hits just kept on coming.

Unfortunately, the attorney's assessment of her father was a bull's eye hit. Sam Logan had forgotten more about horseflesh than most people would ever know, but when it came to taking care of his own financial matters, he'd been a freaking disaster.

As a successful horse trainer and farrier for most of his adult life, Sam's services were often in high demand. The money he made—and sometimes he'd made a substantial amount—he spent freely, living in and for the moment, lending a helping hand to those in need, and letting the future take care of itself.

For the better part of his life, that strategy had worked well for them.

Sam had made a comfortable life for himself and Hope. She'd never gone hungry and always had a roof over her head. Fortunately, Sam's reputation in and around the Kentucky racing circles kept him steadily employed. Their immediate needs and day-to-day expenses were always met, but saving and budgeting had been foreign concepts to her father.

If Sam had the money for something they wanted, he bought it no matter the cost, practicality, or extravagance. If it was a slow time financially, they'd do without until the next windfall hit. After her mother had split when Hope was five, Sam made sure his daughter had whatever she needed and most of what she wanted, and never once made her feel like a burden left behind by a mother who obviously hadn't wanted her.

Instead, Sam had made their life one grand adventure, often piling her into his old blue Ford pickup to go wherever his work took him. Hope had clothes to wear, toys to play with, and horses to ride. Sam had even found a way to pay for what the scholarships and grants didn't cover for Hope to fulfill her dream of becoming a veterinarian. Since Sam seemed to have everything under control, she never had cause to worry.

At least not until he'd fallen ill, and Hope was forced, much to Sam's displeasure, to look after him as well as his finances. That was when she'd gotten her first glimpse at how bad things truly were.

The house was into its second mortgage, and he had no retirement pension save one small life insurance policy. Thankfully, since Sam had spent eight years in the navy, he was eligible for veteran's benefits, which had helped significantly with his medical expenses. Otherwise, his affairs would have been in much worse shape than they were.

"The life insurance he did maintain should cover his final expenses, with a little left over to pay some of the smaller debts," Lucas continued. "He's about five months behind on his mortgage payments, but with the second mortgage he took out, he owes quite a bit more than the house is likely worth."

Leaning forward, the silver-haired attorney who'd been her

father's friend since childhood took Hope's hand. "I tried to get him to let me help him. I wish he'd listened."

Squeezing Lucas's smooth tanned hand, Hope forced herself to smile. "I know you did, but we all know Sam had a mind of his own. He wouldn't bat an eye at giving anyone the shirt off his back, but he'd die before asking for any help for himself."

That was pretty much how her father had lived his entire life. And ultimately, exactly how he'd died.

"It doesn't seem fair, as his sole heir, that you're the one saddled with the consequences of his generous spirit and bull-headed pride, though."

"Well, it's not like I was expecting to hit the mother lode or anything. Don't worry. I'll find a way to take care of all this."

"Can I do anything to help? A loan, perhaps?"

Rising, Hope patted his hand. "That's very kind of you, but I think I'd better try to handle this on my own without incurring any further debt."

Lucas nodded. "All right." He followed her to the door. "But if there is anything I can do, promise you'll let me know."

Hope's smile came easier than she expected. "I promise." She lifted the manila folder of paperwork Lucas had given her. "Thank you. For everything," she added, knowing he'd probably already done far more than was required of him as her father's attorney because of their decades-old friendship.

Still, what a freaking mess! Hope crossed the thick pewter carpet outside Lucas Danforth's cushy corner office. Yep, the old adage, 'when it rains, it pours,' couldn't ring any truer than it did at this moment. Since she couldn't change her predicament, Hope squared her shoulders and made her way to the reception area, where Drew sat waiting. Although she'd assured him she was fully capable of coming to the attorney's office alone, he'd insisted on driving her anyway.

Seemed he could be as bull-headed as she was.

For once, Hope hadn't argued with him. Instead, she'd

simply gathered her jacket and, with an exasperated "Let's go if you're going," tossed over her shoulder at him, she'd stomped out to his pickup.

Now, though Hope would rather cut out her tongue than admit it, relief washed over her at the mere sight of Drew sitting there, thumbing through his phone.

Most men dressed in a chambray shirt, faded Levi's, and scuffed work boots would look conspicuously out of place in the elegantly appointed waiting area. But not Drew Blackwood. Then again, with the quiet self-confidence he exuded naturally, Hope doubted there was a place on earth he would ever look out of place.

Despite her reluctance, Hope realized more women than she could count would give their eye teeth for Drew to accompany them anywhere, even if it were only across the street to a freaking outhouse. Since the day he'd arrived in Kentucky, the effect he'd had on every hopeful female aged eight to eighty was hard to miss and just as difficult to ignore.

And why not? The man was gorgeous with his closely cropped black wavy hair, piercing baby blues, and sexy five o'clock shadow that usually started to emerge somewhere closer to noon. If that combo wasn't lethal enough, throw in his killer smile and smokin' hot body, and it was a miracle that women didn't spontaneously combust in his presence.

Hope remembered the stir that erupted among the female employees when he'd first come to work at Wakefield. She'd been on summer break from her first year of veterinary school, fulfilling some of her field experience hours while working at the clinic.

Not that she'd been immune to his outrageously potent appeal. Far from it. Like every other red-blooded female in a hundred-mile radius, all her girlie parts had stirred to life the instant he walked in the door. And though she spent most of the time around him dizzy with lust, Hope determinedly decided she would not make a fool of herself over the sexy new vet from Virginia.

Besides, like now, her focus had been on her career. She didn't need to get wrapped up in a man, especially not one likely to become her supervisor. Plus, in her experience, relationships in the workplace rarely ended on a happy note. Things became messy, awkward, and complicated to the point that maintaining any semblance of professionalism proved impossible.

Thankfully, their one night together hadn't sullied their working relationship. Yes, the pregnancy did complicate their situation, but so far, they were managing without too many extra hurdles to jump.

"How'd it go?" Drew asked as he slipped into his shearling-lined barn jacket.

"It went." Hope sighed and crossed the marble floor to the bank of elevators. The doors opened before she depressed the down button, and they stepped inside the cubicle.

"That bad, huh?" Drew replied as Hope hit the button for the main floor and sagged against the wall with another heavy sigh.

"Worse." Well, that might be a little harsh, since Hope had halfway expected Lucas to paint a much bleaker picture. With everything else combusting in her world lately, she was grateful for that small favor, at least.

Silently, they headed for Drew's pickup. Once buckled in, he slung his left wrist over the steering wheel, pinning her with his intense blue gaze. "How bad is it?"

And here was Exhibit A for why Hope hadn't wanted him to accompany her today. His persistence. The meeting with her father's attorney had nothing to do with her pregnancy, so what reason did she have to burden him with the results of her father's financial ineptitude? Besides, once she laid everything out and put together a plan, Hope was confident in her ability to handle the situation on her own.

"You've already wasted half your morning, Drew. You certainly don't need to spend any more of your time on the Logan family saga."

"It was my idea to come along, remember."

"Insisted was more like it," Hope shot back more sharply than she intended. On top of her jacked-up hormones, the toll of the last few months had rubbed every one of her nerves completely raw. "Sorry. You didn't deserve that."

"How bad is it?" Drew repeated, the weight of his gaze like lead.

So tenacious. Like a dog with a bone. Might as well tell him what the lawyer revealed. Then, maybe, they could get on with their day. "At least five missed mortgage payments that actually equal ten, since Sam also took out a second mortgage on the house, which means the amount owed far exceeds the actual property value. On top of that, there's about six months' worth of bills he just let go."

"I'm sorry, Hope."

Reluctant to look at him and see the pity in his beautiful blue eyes, Hope toyed with the strap of her purse. "I should have paid more attention. Insisted he see a doctor sooner. Maybe I could have prevented everything from snowballing into this complete and utter disaster."

"You could have been there every day and it wouldn't have mattered. Sam wasn't going to tell you anything he didn't want you to know. He didn't want to worry you with his troubles— even I could see that."

"Yeah, well, his troubles have just become all mine, now, haven't they?"

———

Though Drew hadn't known Hope's father well, his reputation in the racing circle was legendary. Since arriving in Louisville, Drew had seen and heard enough to know Sam Logan was a proud man who always took care of his own, never troubling anyone, least of all his only child, with any of the hardships life dealt him. He'd do whatever needed doing today and take care of tomorrow when it came.

The only problem with Sam's philosophy was that tomorrow had eluded him but was now crashing down on his daughter. Between Drew and her father, neither had done a very good job of protecting and taking care of Hope.

Drew's heart ached at the sorrow shadowing her dark eyes. Like Sam, Hope was someone who readily lent a hand to anyone in need but would never ask any for herself. Even when offered, Hope was reluctant to accept assistance because she didn't want to burden anyone with her problems.

Since her father's illness, Drew had lost count of the times Hope had assured him she was fine and could handle everything on her own. It got to the point he didn't ask or offer anymore. He just did what he thought best, whether she liked it or not. That was what friends did. And regardless of how blurred the lines became due to the pregnancy, Drew still considered Hope one of his best friends.

And he wanted to help her. To be there for her. To lessen her load and erase the sadness stealing the usual sparkle from her beautiful amber eyes. If he didn't think she'd slap him silly, he'd reach across the seat, pull her into his arms, and promise her everything would be all right.

But Hope was her father's daughter, and Drew knew full well her pride wouldn't dare allow him to ride in and save the day. Just because she'd agreed that all decisions regarding the baby would be joint ones in no way meant she was ready for him to jump in and take over her problems.

Still, he needed to do something. "What can I do to help?"

Hope shook her head. "Nothing." She leaned back against the headrest and stared out the front windshield. "First, I need to take a long look at everything and then figure out a plan of action." She drew in a deep breath. "Except all I'd like to do right now is to just put everything out of my mind for a little while." Hope turned her head against the seat to look at him. "How terrible is that?"

"It's not." And it wasn't. With everything Hope had endured the last three and a half months, Drew had little doubt how overwhelmed she must feel. Not to mention how perilously close to the breaking point she had to be after meeting with her father's lawyer. So, taking a break from everything made perfect sense to him. "How about some lunch," Drew suggested as he started the truck.

"You don't have to feed me, Drew. Besides, I've monopolized enough of your time."

"We've already established it was my idea to come with you today. Besides, I have to eat." He lowered his gaze to her belly. "And you definitely need to eat. Seems kind of silly not to eat together," he rationalized and pulled out of the parking lot, heading for Toby's Diner.

A few minutes passed before she broke the silence. "So, I hear Dr. Wakefield made you an offer."

Neil Wakefield had only approached Drew the day before with the idea of them becoming partners in the clinic. "News travels fast."

Although the older vet insisted he had no plans to retire anytime in the foreseeable future, he had promised his wife that when they became grandparents, he'd lessen his load so they could visit with their family more often. For that to occur, Neil needed a reliable partner to oversee the facility's operation in his absence. Someone who shared the same passion and drive he possessed. Someone he could trust.

Totally taken aback by the offer, Drew expressed his gratitude for the opportunity and promised to give the decision the thought and attention it deserved. No rush to answer, Neil had insisted, since their first grandchild wasn't due to arrive until March. Besides, a decision of this magnitude should never be made in haste.

Drew agreed. He was well aware his grandfather was still holding out for Drew to return to Virginia, join his practice, and eventually take over when the old man finally decided to retire. The topic had been something the two of them had talked about frequently after Drew had decided at the ripe old age of twelve that he wanted to be a vet like Pops.

"Do you think you will?" Hope asked. "Become a partner?"

"I'd be a fool not to, don't you think?" It *was* a chance of a lifetime, after all. "And with the baby..." Drew let his voice trail off because even though Hope assured him they'd make decisions regarding the baby together, aside from the day she informed him about the pregnancy, they hadn't discussed the matter further.

"The baby shouldn't make any difference in your choice."

"*Really?*" Drew turned onto the street where the diner was located. "Because I think our child makes a huge difference in every decision we make from this point forward."

"I meant as far as the baby is concerned, it wouldn't matter whether you become a partner or not."

"Especially if you decide not to keep it."

Hope sighed, visibly as well as audibly. "I never said that's what I wanted to do."

"But you're considering it."

"Considering doesn't mean the decision is made, Drew," she reminded him.

True. That was all Neil had asked him to do as well. Consider becoming his partner. Didn't mean that would be his ultimate decision, especially since he did have other options.

Drew eased the truck into an empty spot across from the restaurant and had no more than shut off the engine when his phone vibrated against his hip. Great. Just great. Praying it wasn't a veterinary emergency, Drew removed the device from its holster and looked at the screen.

Pops.

Panic surged through him. "It's my grandfather." Drew looked at Hope. "I need to answer."

"Of course." Hope opened the door and hooked her thumb toward the diner. "I'll go on in and get a table. So, take your time." She hopped out of the truck and closed the door.

Drew swiped the screen to life and brought the phone to his ear. "What's up, old man? Everything all right?" God, he hoped so.

A hearty chuckle reverberated in Drew's ear. "Well, now, that depends on who you're asking, I reckon'. For the most part, I'd say we're all fair to midlin'. Ol' Arthur's been acting up," he confessed, using his time-worn euphemism for arthritis. "Cold weather makes it worse, and we've had a few pretty cool days lately."

"Maybe you should think about slowing down a little."

"Funny you should mention that."

"Oh, are you finally gonna listen to what everybody's been telling you for the past ten years and retire?"

"That, my dear boy, depends a great deal on you."

And here we go.

Ezekiel Elijah Blackwood, or Doc to most everyone but his family, was pushing the hell out of eighty and still working many ten-hour days as a large animal vet for most of the horse and cattle farmers in the northern region of Virginia along with bordering towns in Maryland and the eastern panhandle of West Virginia.

The last time Drew returned to Lone Oaks, the thousand-acre farm his family had owned and operated for three generations, he couldn't help but notice there wasn't as much pep in his grandfather's step as he remembered. For the last several years, everyone in the family had been urging the Blackwood patriarch into retiring, but Zeke kept insisting he simply wasn't ready.

"Rest assured," Pops informed them all, "when the time comes, I'll let you know."

Was that the impetus for this call? Had his grandfather decided he was ready to hang up his stethoscope and overalls? Only one way to find out, Drew guessed. "How does it depend on me?"

"Actually, it depends on whether you accept my proposition."

Of course it did. Drew couldn't help but smile. Since the day he'd decided to follow in his grandfather's footsteps, their plan had been set—once Drew graduated from vet school, he'd return home, join Pops in his practice and take over when Zeke was ready to retire.

And if Drew hadn't been offered the coveted fellowship at Wakefield, that's how his future would've played out. Instead, after a few months of working solely with horses, Drew made the decision to specialize in equine medicine. With its wealth of horseflesh, remaining in Louisville to establish and cultivate his career proved the better choice.

Though clearly disappointed, Pops had agreed with Drew's decision. But he never missed a chance to remind Drew what still waited for him in Beaumont either.

"You're awfully quiet, boy," Zeke interrupted Drew's thoughts. "Guess you've figured out the reason for my call."

"You haven't exactly been subtle about your expectations, Pops."

A deep chuckle rumbled in his ear. "No, I guess I haven't. But I'm not getting any younger, Andrew, and I'd like the chance to talk to you more seriously about coming home to practice."

"Pops..."

"Hear me out, boy. With the holidays bearing down on us —Thanksgiving's what? Two, three weeks away? I'm thinking you can come home for the holidays and see what's what. Plus, it'll give us time to talk things through."

What impeccable timing. First, he finds out he's going to be a father. Then Wakefield offers him a partnership. And now, his grandfather wants him to come home for the holidays to convince him Lone Oaks is where he belongs. Throw in that Hope may decide she wants to give their baby up for adoption, and his life took on a whole other level of complicated.

"I've got a solid practice here, Pops."

"You can have an even more solid practice right here as well."

"But your practice isn't only dedicated to horses." *Nor is it part of a prestigious equine clinic where I could be a partner. But more importantly, it isn't where the mother of my unborn child resides.* How in the world could he consider leaving Louisville for six weeks with Hope pregnant and indecisive?

"The horse industry is growing by leaps and bounds around here. Granted, it's not Louisville or Belmont, but it's a whole lot bigger'n it was. And Pimlico's barely an hour away," he emphasized, referencing the home to the Preakness, the second leg of the Triple Crown.

"I know, but..."

"Now, don't say no until we've talked in person. I'm sure you have some vacation time built up, so how about you come on home for the holidays? While you're here, you can go with me on calls and get a first-hand account of the people as well as the animals. That way, you can make a more informed decision."

Three months ago, this would have been an easier conversation to have with his grandfather. Now, with Hope and the baby combined with the bleak news she'd just received from her father's attorney, there was no way Drew could leave her and go back to Virginia for an extended stay, especially through the holidays.

Her first without her father.

And what about the partnership? If Drew chose to go home after Neil's offer, if only for Thanksgiving and Christmas, what message would that send? That he was fickle?

Ungrateful? Would it cause the elder vet to reconsider his proposition?

Who the hell knew?

"I'm not sure this is the best time to leave Kentucky, Pops."

"Why not? It's the holidays."

"And yesterday, Neil Wakefield asked me to consider becoming his partner at the clinic." Might as well lay it all out there.

"Perfect timing, then. Gives you the chance to see both sides of the coin before you make a decision either way."

Maybe, but still. "You're talking about being away for over a month, Pops." Getting the time off wouldn't be an issue, not at this time of the year, but leaving Hope? No freaking way.

"Yes, but during the slowest time in horse racing," Pops pointed out. "Besides, if Wakefield thinks enough of your abilities to offer you a partnership now, I'm sure he'll welcome you back with open arms if, after giving things a look-see up here, you decide Kentucky is where you want to continue practicing. All I'm asking is that you don't make up your mind until you've given things here a fighting chance."

Apparently, the old man wasn't going to make this easy on him. Or take no for an answer. But what else was new? Zeke Blackwood was not only known for his veterinary acumen but for being a stubborn ol' coot as well.

"Your Mama and Daddy miss you, Andrew. And your grandmother, well, you know how she dotes on you boys. I'm sure you don't want to disappoint all of 'em by not coming home for the holidays again this year, do you?"

Oh, so now he was pulling out the big guns.

"And none of us are getting any younger, you know. Plus, there's Reese. That boy's still struggling with his grief over losing Livvie. Trying to run the farm and raise two motherless little boys isn't easy. Having his brother around would be a boon for him, too, 'specially since the two of you were always so close."

Now, the old man was throwing both shame *and* guilt into the mix. Drew realized he should be in better touch with his family, especially his oldest brother, who'd lost his wife to cancer seven months ago. The last time Drew returned to Lone Oaks had been in April for Olivia's funeral, and since it was prime horse racing season, he hadn't been able to stay as long as he should have.

"Look, son, I know you have a big-time gig down there, but your family's here. Family that needs you right now. Come home for the holidays, Andrew. If after the new year you decide Kentucky is where you want to be, I promise to honor your decision and stop badgering you to come back to join my practice."

Yeah, like that would ever happen as long as there was breath in the old man's body. But how could Drew say no to the rest without seeming heartless and insensitive? Selfish and cold?

"You know, if family isn't enough to entice you to return, Julie Hansen is back in town. I bet your Mama and Grandma would be glad to invite her to some holiday festivities at Lone Oaks."

If Pops thought Julie Hansen was a temptation, he was sorely mistaken. "You trying to get me to come home or run in the opposite direction?"

His grandfather's answer was a booming chuckle.

If Drew needed a reason *not* to return to Virginia, the matchmaking efforts of his mother and grandmother did the trick.

"I'll make you a deal. You agree to my proposition, and I'll see to it the womenfolk refrain from trying to hook you up while you're here."

Like anyone, least of all his grandfather, could control

Anna and Sarah Blackwood when they set their mind to something.

Then, the idea hit him. Why not ask Hope to come to Lone Oaks with him? She could use the time away from Kentucky, the overwhelming memories that would undoubtedly besiege her during Thanksgiving and Christmas, and the plight her father unwittingly bequeathed her. If Hope accompanied Drew to Virginia, he'd be able to honor his grandfather's request, he and Hope wouldn't be six hundred miles apart, and she wouldn't be alone for the two biggest holidays of the year.

At Lone Oaks, she'd be surrounded by not only his parents and grandparents but his three brothers, two nephews, a thousand head of cattle, and a stable full of horses. She could grieve in private while figuring out the best way to handle Sam's financial affairs without the well-intentioned input of her friends, coworkers, and acquaintances. Plus, it would allow the two of them the much-needed time and space to work through everything concerning the baby.

"You still there?" Pops' voice thundered in his ear.

"Yeah. I'm still here." Drew hesitated, knowing full well he needed to give this idea some more thought instead of going with his gut. But what the hell. "Okay, Pops. I'll come home on one condition."

"Name it." Happiness mingled with relief in Zeke's booming baritone.

"I want to bring someone with me."

"Oh really?"

Drew heard the uptick of surprise in Pops' question. "Yeah. Her name is Hope."

"I see," Zeke crooned, and Drew could picture the smile on his grandfather's sun-weathered face.

No, he didn't. Well, at least not all of it. But that was okay. Whether she'd admit it or not, Hope needed this time away. Now, all Drew had to do was convince her to agree.

CHAPTER THREE

"Sorry. That took longer than I expected." Drew slid onto the red vinyl seat across from Hope. He rested his elbows on the chrome-edged Formica table and scrubbed his hands over his face.

"Is everything okay?" Hope asked, concern lacing her voice.

"Yeah. Pops just tends to get long-winded sometimes."

Cupping her water glass, Hope lowered her gaze. "Be glad you're still able to talk to your family."

The bleakness in Hope's voice clawed at Drew's heart, which only reinforced his decision to bring her home with him. Though his family could be overwhelming at times, Drew truly believed Lone Oaks was where Hope needed to be.

"My grandfather wants me to come home for the holidays."

Hope looked up from stirring the ice with her straw. "You should go."

"Trying to get rid of me?"

"No."

Of course not. Her response was about spending valued time with his family while he still had the chance. Time Hope wished she still had with her father. "It's a long time to be away. About six weeks."

Looking at him, Hope shrugged. "So?"

"Well, for one, it's not just for a visit." Drew leaned back against the booth. "I think I've mentioned that growing up, the plan was that when I finished vet school, I'd return home to join my grandfather's practice and take over when he retires."

"But then you got the fellowship at Wakefield."

"Right." Drew nodded. "Which wasn't something either of us factored into the master plan. Pops accepted it was an opportunity I couldn't pass up, but I know he's been disappointed at how long I've stayed here."

"And now he thinks it's time for you to go home?"

Drew nodded again. "Since he'll turn eighty next fall, I think he's about ready to hang up his stethoscope. He wants me to come home for Thanksgiving and Christmas. While there, I can work with him in order to make a more informed decision about whether to stay at Wakefield or partner with him."

"Did you tell him about Dr. Wakefield's offer?"

"Yeah, but instead of backing off, it only re-enforced his resolve. He said now it was even more important to weigh the options before making a decision of this magnitude about the future of my career."

"He's right."

Maybe so. But before Drew could respond, Rosie Butler appeared in her cuffed short-sleeved pink uniform with a white scalloped apron tied around her tiny waist. "What can I get you to drink, Doc?" she asked Drew in her raspy three-pack-a-day drawl.

"Just iced tea for me, Rosie."

"Y'all ready to order?" she asked, her attention redirected to Hope.

"I think I'll have a bowl of Toby's vegetable soup and a grilled cheese, please."

"Sounds good," Drew agreed with a smile. "Make it two."

Pulling a pencil from the brown nest of hair piled atop her head, Rosie jotted down their orders. "Be right back with your tea." Again, she turned her attention toward Hope, her bottle-green eyes full of warmth and heartfelt sympathy. "You want anything else, honey?"

With a forced smile, Hope shook her head. "I'm good. Thanks, Rosie."

The wand-thin waitress gave Hope's arm a motherly squeeze as she headed toward the pass behind the counter to deliver their orders.

"I wish everyone would stop treating me like I'm an orphan or something."

"Sam had a lot of friends. They care about you and share your loss."

"I know." Sighing, Hope took a sip of her water. "But it still makes me uncomfortable. I don't want anyone's pity."

Drew laid his hand over hers and considered it a small victory when she didn't pull away. "I don't think anyone pities you, Hope. They're concerned about you and want to reach out. To be there if you need anything." Like me, Drew refrained from adding.

"I know," she repeated. "It's just hard is all."

Rosie appeared with Drew's tea. She slid a straw from her pocket and laid it on the table. "Food'll be up in a minute," she promised before turning on her crepe-soled heel toward the counter.

Drew peeled the paper off the straw and dunked it into his tea. Though he'd already told his grandfather he'd come home as long as he could bring Hope with him, he was beginning to wonder if leaving Kentucky right now was really for the best. He looked up at Hope. "If I do go back for the holidays, what kind of message do you think that will send to Dr. Wakefield?"

"That you want to spend the holidays with your family?" She continued to swirl the ice with her straw. "Most people do. Including Dr. Wakefield. So I'm pretty sure he'll understand."

"Good point." In fact, hadn't Neil insisted he not rush? To take his time and not make his decision in haste?

Returning, Rosie set two steaming bowls of soup and a plate of grilled cheese sandwiches between them. "Let me know if y'all need anything else."

Taking a sandwich, Drew tore it in half and dipped it in his soup. "When I was younger, being a vet like Pops and becoming his partner was my dream." He smiled ruefully. "My only dream, actually."

"But getting the fellowship changed your mind?"

"I'm not sure it changed my mind, but it opened up another opportunity I hadn't considered. One where I could work solely with horses."

Hope blew on her spoonful of soup. "That's not a possibility in Virginia?"

"Not exclusively. But the industry is expanding." He took a long pull of his iced tea. "Like I said, Pops wants me to come home and work with him before making a final decision. Throw in the holidays and how I haven't spent many at home for the last few years, and his argument is pretty tight."

"Then you should definitely go."

————

It might not be her place to give Drew advice on what he should or shouldn't do, but if Hope had a loving family somewhere who wanted her to be with them for the holidays, she wouldn't be able to get there fast enough.

In fact, Hope envied Drew's connection with his family. All those people who loved him and wanted him back in their close-knit circle. She understood what it was like to be loved like that because, no matter what, Hope never once doubted her father would have moved heaven and earth for her. A quiet man, Sam hadn't voiced the words very often, but not a day went by when he hadn't shown Hope she was the light of his life.

Now he was gone, leaving her so profoundly alone.

Hope looked up. "Trust me, Drew, you don't want any regrets."

He shook his head. "No. I don't."

"Then what's holding you back?"

"Six weeks is a long time to be away."

"That's just an excuse."

One dark brow arched. "You think?"

"You know it is." Hope tore off a small piece of her sandwich. "Aside from emergencies, this is a slow time in the horse business. The rest of us at the clinic can handle everything in your absence." She met his gaze. "So go. Enjoy this time with your family, Drew. Because once it's gone, it's not something you can ever get back."

"What about the baby?"

"I'll still be pregnant after the holidays." A sharp pang shot through her. The holidays. Good heavens, how was she ever going to make it through the holidays without Sam?

Or Drew.

Though she'd valiantly tried to resist, Hope had come to rely on Drew being there for her these past few months. She'd grown accustomed to having him around to watch out for her. Making sure she ate and got enough rest. Insisting she take precautions and didn't overdo anything.

Still, going home as his grandfather wanted was definitely something Drew needed to do.

"You could come with me."

Hope blinked her surprise. "What?" She must have misheard him.

"You could come to Lone Oaks with me."

"Have you lost your mind?" What other explanation was there?

"No." He shook his head, emphasizing his point. "Think about it. Earlier, you said you'd like to put all this stuff with your father's finances out of your mind for a little while. This would give you the perfect opportunity to do that. Plus, the first holiday season without a loved one is usually the hardest. With Thanksgiving and Christmas coming so close to Sam's passing, everything will be magnified and more difficult. If you come home with me, you won't have reminders everywhere you turn, and it'll give you time to get your bearings and make a plan for how to handle everything after the new year."

Drew smiled, adding, "Besides that, we'd have time to figure things out where the baby is concerned without being under the watchful eye of everyone we know and work with here."

"Just your family's watchful eyes."

"But they wouldn't know."

"No one here knows," Hope pointed out.

"But they will," he countered. "It's not something we can keep hidden for very much longer."

He was right about that. Each day her jeans were getting more difficult to fasten and more uncomfortable to wear.

"I don't know." Although his points were valid, Hope still harbored quite a few reservations.

"By coming along, you'd also be saving me from my mother and grandmother's relentless matchmaking. With you there, maybe they won't feel so compelled to focus on hooking me up with every unattached female in a fifty-mile radius."

"Likely because they'll assume *we've* already hooked up."

His grin was quick. And lethal. "Well, we kind of have."

True. "It's not exactly the same."

"It's not all that different either." His expression grew serious, and his next words clutched at something deep inside her. "I want you to come with me, Hope. We can enjoy the holidays, gather our thoughts, and take things one day at a time while we make some pretty important decisions about the future."

If only it were that easy. "That all sounds very nice, Drew, but there's one important component you haven't considered."

His dark brows knitted together. "What's that?"

"My job. Not only do I have my own bills to pay, but now, I also have my father's debts to contend with. Don't you think it would be rather careless and irresponsible of me to take a month off work while all the debt continues piling up?"

"You have paid vacation days you probably haven't used. I'm sure we can work something out to combine what's owed to you so that you can take the time off."

"I can't just walk away from everything here, Drew."

"It's only for six weeks."

"Oh, so, now, it's *only* six weeks. When it was just *you* going, six weeks was a *long* time."

A grin twinkled in his eyes. "I exaggerated."

Hope was tempted. *Really* tempted. To get away. Forget about everything for a while. Rest, regroup, rejuvenate.

But she couldn't. Not in good conscience. Leaving with Drew and avoiding her obligations would be irresponsible. Besides, the rumor mill would run amok. "Can you imagine what our coworkers, let alone Dr. Wakefield, will think if I turn my back on everything here and go home with you for six weeks?"

"Probably the same thing they're going to think when you start to show."

Shit! Definitely no argument there. "But they wouldn't automatically know you're the father."

"I'm not going to lie to anybody about being the father of this baby, Hope."

Of course not. And Hope couldn't blame him. In fact, if anything, his tenacity made her respect him even more.

"Besides, I already told my grandfather I was bringing you with me."

Shocked, Hope leaned forward. "You did what?" Asking her to come home with him had surprised her enough, but confessing he'd informed his grandfather he was bringing her before even asking her, well, that completely threw Hope for a loop.

And to tell the truth, she wasn't quite sure how she felt about it.

Drew shrugged his mile-wide shoulders. "What was I supposed to do, Hope? He's pleading with me, pulling out all the stops—guilting and shaming me about not going back as often as I should. My whole family's there, and I always have a reason why I can't go home, even for the holidays."

"What's that got to do with me?"

"Because this time, you're the reason for me to stay here."

"Because of the baby." Why else? Still, her heart leapt a little at his response.

"Yes," Drew admitted. "But also because of *you*."

His words snatched the breath right out of her lungs. Speechless, Hope just shook her head and stared wide-eyed at Drew. She was completely thunderstruck. Flabbergasted. And so incredibly touched.

Damn him!

"I owe it to my family to come home, but I won't go and leave you here alone for the first holidays without your father."

A vise-like grip tightened Hope's chest. She couldn't let him do this. She couldn't be the reason he didn't spend the holidays with his family. "I won't be alone. I have friends. People I've known my entire life. I'll be fine."

Even as the last three words left her mouth, Hope knew they were a lie. As much as she hated to admit it, she wouldn't be fine. Not only would she miss her father like crazy, but she'd also miss Drew more than she was ready to admit.

To him, at least.

"Maybe *I* won't be fine," Drew responded, his gaze intense as he linked his fingers atop the table and leaned forward. "What will it take for you to agree to come home with me for the holidays, Hope? Name it. I'll do anything."

Wow. Hope certainly hadn't expected those words to come out of his mouth. Or the tingly warmth radiating through every cell in her body as a result. Part of her realized it would be a relief of sorts to go with Drew. But the other, more rational part remembered all the responsibilities she'd leave behind as if she didn't have a care in the world.

Yet, Drew did have a point. The holidays, especially the first ones, would be beyond brutal without Sam. Although he loved all the holidays, Christmas was her father's absolute favorite.

Each year, on the day after Thanksgiving, they'd trudge through the woods to find the perfect tree. Once they dragged it home and set it up, Sam would haul out the boxes of decorations they'd accumulated over the years. They'd spend the rest of the day and most of the evening decorating the entire house while singing along, mostly off-key, to the Christmas songs playing on the ancient stereo her father had refused to upgrade. He insisted vinyl recordings were much better than anything digitized.

With Sam, the holidays were a magical time. And it had little to do with wrapped gifts under the tree. Hope never cared about material things. Instead, what she cherished most was sharing the wonder, excitement, and joy of the season with her father.

Her heart broke even further to realize Sam would never get to create those same memories with his grandchild. Maybe that was why she wasn't sure about keeping the baby. That and the incessant fear that she'd turn out like her mother.

Everything was so freaking complicated. Her father's death, his overwhelming financial woes, the new life growing inside her, and the ultimate curve ball Drew had just thrown into the mix by inviting her to go home with him for the holidays.

If she were the impulsive sort, Hope would be packing right now instead of analyzing the situation to death, fearing she wasn't acting responsibly or doing the right thing. But maybe, just this once, it would be okay to exercise a little spontaneity in the name of self-preservation. To allow herself some much-needed time and space to go through the grieving process and sort through her options without the well-meaning input or suggestions from Sam's long-time friends and associates as well as her own.

Where she could just *be* for a little while.

Would that be selfish of her? Negligent? Careless?

Hell no, girl. It's called survival. Hope could hear her father's assurance as if he were sitting right there beside her in the booth.

"Hope?" Drew's voice broke into her thoughts. "Are you okay?"

Yeah, she was. For now, anyway. "I'm fine," she answered a little more confidently than she felt. "And you don't have to do anything."

A smile tugged at his lips. "Does that mean..."

"That I'll go home with you for the holidays?" When Drew nodded, so did Hope. "Yes, that's what it means."

"Really?"

Hope nodded again. "Yeah. Really."

———

An hour later, Drew dropped Hope at her townhouse to change clothes for their afternoon shift. As soon as she closed the door behind her, he realized what a huge freaking risk he was taking by leaving her alone so soon after she'd finally agreed to go home with him for the holidays. Hell, by now, she'd likely reconsidered his offer and decided she couldn't accept his invitation.

Maybe he should have waited and driven her back to the clinic. Then, he could have run interference when she began her litany of reasons why she really needed to remain in Kentucky after all. Yet, if he'd stayed with her, Drew would lose the opportunity to speak privately with Dr. Wakefield about taking her to Virginia for over a month.

Which brought up another concern: How would the senior vet react to Drew's request for a six-week leave of absence less than forty-eight hours after offering him a full partnership in the clinic? Would Wakefield be insulted? Offended? Or would he understand Drew's need to honor his grandfather's request, especially since if it weren't for Pops, Drew wouldn't be a veterinarian in the first place?

Furthermore, Drew didn't only owe his grandfather; he owed it to himself. And with Hope along, the only thing it would cost was time. Plus, it would make Pops and the rest of his family happy.

"Maryann said you wanted to see me." In his late fifties, Neil Wakefield was a strapping man with thinning blond hair and keen blue eyes.

Drew looked up from his computer screen to where the seasoned vet was leaning against the doorjamb. "Yeah. You have a few minutes?"

"Sure." Stepping into the modestly furnished office, Neil closed the door and crossed the mottled gray tile. "What's up?" he asked as he dropped into one of the black leather chairs facing Drew's long walnut desk.

Might as well jump in with both feet. "I got a call from my grandfather this morning."

"Everything okay?" His concern was genuine.

"Yeah." Drew pulled in a deep breath and relayed his conversation with Pops to Neil.

"I'm assuming you agreed."

His response was encouraging, at least. "Seems like the right thing to do. I'll be able to appease my grandfather and spend some time with my family."

"It'll also provide you an opportunity to consider all your options before making any decisions about your future." He inclined his head. "And where you want to practice."

"That's what Pops said."

"He's right."

Second time he'd heard that today. Drew ran a hand over his jaw. "I don't want you to think I'm not taking your offer seriously. Or that I'm ungrateful in any way."

"I know that." Neil grinned. "But I'm also not going to ease your conscience." His expression sobered. "I'd hate to lose you here at Wakefield."

"I honestly have no idea what'll happen with this trip. I love working here, and the thought of leaving is daunting as hell. But Virginia is my home, and if it weren't for my grandfather, I never would have ventured into veterinary medicine at all. I feel obligated to at least honor his request to work with him for a few weeks before making a decision."

"Of course." The lack of hesitation in Neil's response comforted Drew. "Like I said, I'd hate like hell to lose you, but family should always come first."

"Six weeks is a long furlough, though."

"Not really. It's not foaling season, and the clinic will be operating on an abbreviated schedule in December anyway. I'm sure you have enough leave accumulated."

Since he rarely took any time off, that much was true. "There is one other thing."

Neil arched a brow. "I'm listening."

"It's about Hope. I thought it might be good for her to come with me. Get her away from all the reminders for a little while, especially during her first holidays without her father."

"I agree. But you know as well as I do that Hope will argue

till she's blue in the face she'll be just fine and doesn't need any special treatment."

"Actually, I talked to her earlier, and believe it or not, she agreed to go with me."

Astonished, Neil leaned forward. "You're kidding."

Drew shook his head. "No. Shocked the hell out of me, too. Of course, by now, I'm sure she's come up with a million reasons why it's a bad idea and has changed her mind."

"Then we'll just have to double team her because you're right, she needs some time away," Neil replied. "So, what time-frame are you considering?"

"I thought we'd leave a day or two before Thanksgiving and stay until New Year's Day."

With a nod, Neil rose from the chair and turned to leave. When he reached the door, he paused. "I know this is none of my business, but you're good for Hope, Drew. Personally, as well as professionally. Sam would appreciate you looking out for her."

"Neil, I..."

The older vet shook his head. "I'm not prying into your business. Just making an observation."

"I appreciate it." And he did.

"If you need any help convincing Hope not to change her mind, you know where to find me."

CHAPTER FOUR

For about the bazillionth time in the last three weeks, Hope wondered if she'd completely lost her mind for even considering, let alone actually accepting Drew's invitation to go home with him for the holidays.

Yes, she had been through a rough couple of months. Losing her father had been devastating, and Hope knew her first holiday season without Sam was bound to be excruciatingly painful. Then, there was his financial disaster she felt responsible for clearing up. And to top everything off, she was carrying her boss's child.

All circumstances she should deal with on her own. In Louisville. Like the grownup she was.

By going to Virginia with Drew, Hope was only postponing the inevitable. When the holidays were over and she returned to Kentucky, her situation would be the same. Her father would still be gone. The bills would still be waiting to be paid. Everyone who knew her and her father would continue to pity her.

And she'd still be pregnant with Drew Blackwood's baby.

In hindsight, the most logical solution was to stay where she belonged. To face the music of life without her father and move forward as best she could. Yes, it would be hard, but hard wasn't impossible.

Yet, logic apparently reigned supreme over both her conscience and whacked-out hormones, because here she sat, strapped into the passenger seat of Drew's heavy-duty pickup as he sped down the highway. And while Lynyrd Skynyrd proclaimed their love for Alabama through the stereo system, Hope wondered what the hell she was going to do with herself in Virginia for the next six weeks.

Of course, nothing in their agreement said she needed to stay the entire time. If Hope wanted to return to Louisville sooner than Drew, she'd just book a flight or rent a car and go home.

"You're awfully quiet over there," Drew broke the silence that had stretched between them for the last thirty minutes.

"Just thinking," Hope replied.

"Please tell me you aren't still second-guessing your decision to come with me."

Hope gave him a sidelong glare. "You know I am." No use holding back the truth.

His glance in her direction was brief but potent. "I wish you wouldn't."

Really? How could she not? Basically, she was running away from her personal and professional obligations. Leaving her colleagues to pick up her slack once again. If those weren't reasons enough, what were people going to think about the two of them taking off together for the holidays?

For six freaking weeks.

Hope cringed. No doubt the scuttlebutt was already buzzing among their friends and coworkers. Speculation would be raised and conclusions drawn. Hell, she'd be surprised if pools hadn't been generated to take bets on everything from whether they were more than friends to Drew's opting to remain at the equine clinic or leave to join his grandfather's practice.

"Coming to Virginia with me is not that big a deal."

"That's easy for you to say. You're going home. I'm going somewhere I've never been before. To spend two of the most celebrated holidays in the world with people I've never met." Realizing how ungrateful she sounded, Hope quickly added, "No offense."

"None taken." A grin eased into Drew's whisker-stubbled cheeks. "Trust me when I tell you none of my family will be strangers for very long. The minute your feet hit Lone Oaks soil, you'll be welcomed with open arms and treated like they've known you forever."

"You sound pretty confident about that."

"I am," Drew assured her. "Now, don't get me wrong. They can be quite an overwhelming bunch, but their hearts are in the right place." He grinned again, causing her stomach to dip and dive. "I did ask them to dial their fervor down a notch or six, though."

"Thanks." Despite the tangle of knots twisting inside her belly, Hope *was* grateful. For everything Drew had done and continued to do on her behalf, whether she needed him to or not. "I just don't want to be a disruption to your family's holiday traditions."

Drew shook his head. "You won't be." He looked at her and smiled. "You'll just become a part of them."

Not exactly words to ease her ever-increasing concerns.

Still, worrying about things out of her control wouldn't change a thing, so Hope decided to channel her angst more constructively by inquiring about Drew's family and where he grew up. With at least ten more hours of driving ahead of them, it would not only pass the time but also help Hope gather more information about Drew and his family before meeting the Blackwood clan.

"Okay." Hope shifted in her seat to face Drew. "Since you pretty much already know my life story and have seen where I grew up, let's use our time wisely by you filling me in on yours."

Drew turned down the radio. "What do you want to know?"

"Tell me about Lone Oaks."

"Not much to tell really. It's a horse and cattle farm that sits on about a thousand acres in northern Virginia. The area is a lot like what we have in Kentucky."

"Including the hills and valleys?"

Drew nodded. "Lone Oaks is located more in the valley region, but we have some spectacular views of the Blue Ridge Mountains."

That was a definite plus, for sure. Hope preferred seeing trees and farmland when she looked out the window rather than steel and concrete.

"Since we're only about seventy miles from the nation's capital, Beaumont and Sheridan have sort of become bedroom communities of DC. Some even consider the area part of the metropolitan suburbs."

"Doesn't sound like you're a big fan of the urban sprawl." Which was understandable. Hope wouldn't be either.

"No. Not really." He shrugged his massive shoulders. "But, aside from the land on Lone Oaks, there really isn't much we can do about it. Fortunately, things haven't gotten too out of hand. As you'll see, the area still has a small-town appeal."

After agreeing to accompany Drew home to Virginia, Hope had done a quick Google search of the area. She found that both Beaumont and Sheridan were municipalities in Beaumont County, which bordered Maryland and West Virginia. Both towns were a part of the region known as Hickory Ridge. The pictures included on the website were absolutely gorgeous.

Hope couldn't wait to see everything up close and in person.

"I think you'll like it," Drew said as if he'd been reading her mind.

Nodding, Hope settled more comfortably in the passenger seat. "So, what about your family? You're one of four boys, correct?"

"Yes." He signaled left to pass a tow truck. "Reese is the oldest. Then me. We're Irish twins, both born in the same year."

"And Reese is the one who lost his wife to cancer?" She remembered him going home for her memorial service.

"Yes. Olivia. Just this past April."

Sadness tugged at Hope's heart. "And he has two boys?"

"Alex and Zach. They're seven and five."

So young to be motherless. Absently, her hand covered her abdomen where her own child grew and emotion welled up in her throat. "That's so sad for all of them," she managed to reply.

"Yeah. It is."

Hearing the grief in Drew's voice sliced straight through Hope. Instinctively, she laid her hand on his forearm and squeezed. As soon as her palm touched his sleeve, warmth rocketed through her, and Hope couldn't help but wonder if Drew felt it too.

Don't be ridiculous! she chided herself. She'd probably only imagined she felt something anyway. Being pregnant had shifted her nervous system and hormones into extreme over-drive, magnifying her emotions and senses a thousand-fold. It was enough to drive her to distraction.

Like right now, trapped in a moving vehicle with the man who seemed to elicit all these warm, tingly feelings inside her. Hope dropped her hand and forced her thoughts back on track and continued with her get-to-know-the-Blackwood-family questions. "What about your other two brothers?"

"Jack is number three. He's two years younger and is a writer."

Right. JD Blackwood, best-selling author of suspense thrillers. Hope had just finished his latest novel, *The Doctor's*

Wife, which debuted at number one on the New York Times Bestseller's List. "I can't put his books down."

"Please don't tell him that. His ego is big enough as it is," Drew replied good-naturedly.

"I'll try to keep my fan-girl suppressed when he's around." Yeah, right. He might be Drew's brother, but he was also a celebrated author. Not to mention one of Hope's favorites. She'd keep that to herself, though. "That brings us to the fourth Blackwood brother."

"Holden." Drew changed lanes to pass an RV from Missouri. "He runs his own construction company."

Hope curled her left leg under her right thigh. "Shew. Four boys. You think your mother was trying for a girl?"

His broad shoulders lifted and fell in a shrug, the gesture tightening the fabric of his blue knit shirt and causing a riot in all her girlie parts. Dang!

"She never said so, but I guess it's possible."

Okay, get yourself under control, Hope chastised herself. No need to make this long trek unbearable. Best to get back to her inquiry. "Does everyone but you live at Lone Oaks?"

"Yeah. Dad and Reese do most of the farming; however, my father is also a lawyer. My grandfather was adamant his children would have college degrees. Dad went to law school, and his sister, my Aunt Clarissa, who also lives in Beaumont, is a nurse. Her husband, Earl, is Dad's law partner. Family law mainly, but Uncle Earl has done some litigation."

"Your grandparents still live on the farm?"

"Yeah. Soon after Reese was born, they built a smaller house and turned the main house over to my parents."

"And your brothers live there as well?"

"Reese does now. Makes it easier for our mother to help with the boys. But he also has a house he built after he and Livvie were married. Jack has a place on an adjacent piece of land he bought after selling his first book. And Holden's place is a continual work in progress."

"Too busy building homes for others to spend time on his own," Hope supposed.

"Something like that."

Hope propped her elbow on the back of the seat and leaned her head against her fist. "I'm curious. How did you explain bringing me home with you to this big family of yours?"

"I just told Pops I was bringing you along."

"And he just said 'okay'?"

"Actually, his exact words were, 'I see.'"

"That's it?" Hope asked, assuming his grandfather would require more of an explanation.

"That's it," Drew confirmed.

"And he just accepted it? No questions asked?"

"He really didn't have much choice."

"Drew!"

He barked out a laugh. "What? He's getting what he wants. I'm coming home to follow him around for over a month, so he can do everything in his power to persuade me to stay and join his practice."

With all the other happenings in her life the past few weeks, Hope hadn't given much thought to the fact that after the new year, Drew could decide Hickory Ridge was where he belonged. The realization now left a hollow ache in the vicinity of her heart.

But it was his life. Ultimately his decision. And he needed to do what was best for him and his family.

Besides, Virginia was Drew's home, just like Kentucky was hers. If she decided to keep the baby, no law said they needed to live in the same city. Plenty of people with children resided in different states, and everything worked out perfectly for everyone involved.

No reason their situation should differ.

Right?

"Do you think you will?" Hope surprised herself by asking.

His brow crinkled. "Will what?"

"Stay and join your grandfather's practice?" All things considered, Hope thought it a valid question.

Drew shook his head. "I really don't know."

Of course he didn't. Who would when presented with two such auspicious yet vastly different choices? A partnership offer at a prestigious equine facility was a rare, once-in-a-lifetime opportunity. But so was the chance to work alongside the man who inspired his childhood dream of becoming a veterinarian. Both priceless options deserved much thought and consideration.

Hope was glad the decision wasn't hers to make.

"Now I have a question for you," Drew stated.

"Oh-kay." Hope drew out the word, wondering what Drew was going to ask and bracing herself to hear it.

"It's about the baby."

She had a feeling. "What about the baby?"

"Are we gonna tell my family that you're pregnant?"

"You haven't told them?" Hope had just assumed it was something he would have already shared.

Drew slid a glance in her direction. "I haven't told anyone."

Hope shook her head. "Me neither." Not that she had anyone to tell, but Drew—he had a whole flipping family. Why hadn't he said anything to them? Especially his parents. "Do you not want to tell them?"

"Of course I want to tell them."

"But?"

He passed a few more vehicles. "I'll be honest, Hope. They'll have a hard time accepting you may want to give the baby up for adoption."

She figured as much. If Sam were alive, he'd feel the same way. God, she wished she had a crystal ball to see into the future. Then everything would be so much simpler. "Do we have to decide right now?"

"No. But it is something we'll have to decide sooner rather than later."

Hope nodded. "I know." And she did. Another thought hit her. "You have told someone besides your grandfather about me coming home with you, haven't you?"

Devilment twinkled in his oh-so-blue eyes. "Pops probably told half the county before I even made it inside the diner that day."

Hope's eyes flew open. "We're not just going to show up without you having at least told your mother, are we?"

Drew grinned, and Hope's insides trembled. "I like to keep them on their toes."

"Drew!"

"Relax." He took her hand and squeezed it. "I've talked to my mother as well as my father, grandmother, and one of my brothers."

"Only one of your brothers?"

"Jack's in deep-level writing mode on his latest novel, so communicating with him is futile, and Reese is still just trying to get through each day."

She couldn't even imagine. Though Hope suspected how difficult the holidays would be for her without Sam, she couldn't fathom how heartbreaking the first holidays without his wife would be for Reese. Or for his little boys without their mother.

At least she had thirty years of wonderful memories with her father. Reese and his sons were only given a painfully short time with Olivia. Emotion welled up inside Hope for their loss, her eyes puddling as a result. "We'll have to do whatever we can to brighten their holidays," Hope decided out loud. It was the least she could do while imposing on his family.

Drew squeezed her hand again. "Yeah. We will."

Before she became a blubbering idiot, Hope cleared her throat and switched back to what they'd been discussing before. "So, what reason did you give your family for bringing me along with you?"

"The truth. That you've been through a rough couple of months, culminating with the loss of your father, and that you could benefit from some time away. They all thought it was a great idea."

"And they don't think it's the least bit weird for you to just show up with some strange woman they've never met? For six weeks and over the two biggest holidays of the year?"

His eyes glittered. "I didn't know you were strange."

With a roll of her eyes, Hope punched him in the arm. "Ha. Ha."

Devilment twinkled in his baby blues. "Well," he elongated the word, getting back to her question. "I imagine they've drawn a few conclusions of their own."

Hope arched a brow. "Which are?" As if she couldn't guess.

"That we're more than coworkers. Or even friends." His eyes sparkled even brighter. "They may even suspect we're involved." He held up a finger before she could interrupt. "Which we are."

"Only not in the way they'll assume."

"Making a baby with you didn't happen without some intense involvement between us, Hope. Several times if I remember correctly." His lips curved wickedly, the gesture crinkling the corners of his beautiful blue eyes. "And despite the tequila shots, I have a pretty clear memory of our time together."

"It was just one night." Yet one she also remembered quite well.

"But incredible nonetheless."

Heat suffused her cheeks. Intense was quite an understatement regarding what transpired in her bedroom with Drew that night. Mind-boggling. Bone-melting. Heart-stopping. Earth-shattering. Now, those were some more accurate descriptors of what had occurred between them sixteen weeks ago.

No point in reliving what she couldn't let happen again. "I don't want to mislead them, Drew."

"How about we just take things one day at a time?" he suggested. "I promise I won't let them make things uncomfortable for you."

Although she trusted Drew to do his best to keep his promise, after what he'd told her about his mother and grandmother being relentless matchmakers, Hope knew if they found out about the baby, all bets were off.

Lord help her.

CHAPTER FIVE

Eleven hours and twenty-nine minutes after leaving Louisville, Drew passed the sign welcoming them to Beaumont. They'd made good time with only a few pit stops to relieve themselves, stretch, and grab a bite to eat.

Hope was an excellent traveling companion. Despite being pregnant, she didn't need to pee every five minutes, wasn't finicky about their dining options, and even offered to drive if he needed a break or wanted to rest.

After their initial discussion about his family, her visit, and how they'd handle everyone's likely assumptions about their relationship, they'd talked about their work at the clinic, memories of holidays past, and a host of other general get-to-know-each-other-better topics. For the last hour, they'd played a trivia game Hope had found on her phone.

From that, Drew decided they both were veritable founts of totally useless information.

So far, the trip from Kentucky to northern Virginia had been both pleasurable and informative. Drew learned things about Hope he might not have had the opportunity to glean otherwise. Like she loved the color turquoise, enjoyed the most eclectic taste in music, and was not a fan of science fiction. At. All.

If they hadn't made this trip together, Drew would never have discovered how the scent of vanilla he'd noticed clinging to the interior of his truck the past few months was all Hope. He didn't know if it was perfume or lotion or something else entirely, but whatever it was, when Drew inhaled, a sense of comfort, familiarity, and peace enveloped him like an old friend.

Just being in her company had the same effect. Looking at her beautiful face. Gazing into her big doe-like brown eyes. Listening to the smoky sound of her voice when she talked. Sitting close enough for their legs or shoulders to brush. Being near Hope made Drew feel more alive.

Energized.

Whole.

As Drew turned between the stone pillars and drove under the Lone Oaks iron arch, he resisted the urge to take hold of Hope's hand. Instead, he continued down the oak-lined drive. An abundance of lights from a host of buildings illuminated the darkness. Centered on about five acres and amidst an outcropping of buildings, barns, and sheds sat a beautiful two-story log and stacked stone farmhouse with a multitude of gleaming windows and a spacious wraparound porch.

"Welcome to Lone Oaks, Hope."

Her eyes nearly swallowed her beautiful face. "It's huge."

Drew stopped the truck in front of a split rail fence encircling the enormous front and back yards. "A family our size needs a lot of space."

"Is this where your parents live?"

"Yeah. Reese's house is about a quarter-mile farther down, and my grandparents' about a half mile past him." He shut off the engine. "Holden's place is in between, and Jack lives closest to Lake Sheridan."

When Hope smiled, warmth spread through him like sweet honey. "You've got your own Blackwood compound."

"Seems that way sometimes."

Somewhere near the West Virginia-Kentucky border, Hope had braided her hair on either side of her oval face, the banded ends falling just below her shoulders. Except for a swipe of Chapstick frequently applied during the drive, she hadn't bothered with any other makeup. Still, her skin glowed, and her brown eyes sparkled like chocolate diamonds.

Drew had a sudden urge to reach across the console and kiss her. Hard. Instead, he pulled in a deep breath and pushed open his door. If he didn't soon get a grip on his libido, this trip was going to be the longest six weeks of his life. "We'd better head inside before they all descend on us out here."

Hopping out of the truck, Drew made his way around the hood just as Hope closed the passenger door. Hesitating, she began to gnaw on her bottom lip. "It's gonna be okay," Drew reassured her. He draped his arm across her shoulders, pulling her against his side but stopping short of pressing a kiss to her temple. No need to ratchet her anxiety level any higher than it already was.

Especially before they even made it inside the main house.

"That's easy for you to say. They're your family," Hope pointed out as they stepped apart.

"C'mon. The sooner we get inside, the sooner you'll see there's no reason to worry." Drew smiled down at her. "Promise."

They had no more than stepped onto the wraparound porch when both heavy wooden front doors swung open. "It's Uncle Drew and his girlfriend," his nephew, Zach, yelled over his shoulder before turning his bright blue eyes back in their direction. "Hi, Uncle Drew."

Drew ruffled the boy's dark hair. "Hey yourself, Zach."

Not wanting to be left out, the wolf-like dog at the five-year-old's side barked sharply. "Hey there, Sadie," Drew crooned, giving her a brisk rub that turned her arctic eyes into warm pools of pure adoration.

"Are you here all by yourself, Zach?" Drew asked as he led Hope inside.

Awed, Hope stepped onto the gray slate covering the foyer. To her left was a huge great room complete with a vaulted ceiling, exposed wooden beams, and wide-planked hickory floor covered in part by an oblong braided rug in southwestern colors. A fire crackled in the massive stone fireplace situated in front of a grouping of buttery soft leather sofas and recliners draped with what appeared to be handmade afghans and throws.

Immediately, it felt like home.

"Nah. Gram's in the bath—"

"Gram's right here," a feminine voice interrupted as a lovely woman appeared, a smile beaming across her heart-shaped face. "Drew," she sighed happily before pulling him into a welcoming, so-glad-you're-finally-here hug.

A lump lodged itself in Hope's throat when Drew embraced his mother as tightly as she held onto him, her elation at having her son home, where Hope imagined his mother believed he belonged, obvious. Then, easing back slightly, she framed his face with her hands, stood on her tiptoes, and kissed him soundly.

Hope's heart melted completely.

Fortunately, she was saved from becoming a blubbering idiot over the effect Drew's homecoming was having on her when his mother turned toward her, a warm smile, very much like Drew's, lighting her deep brown eyes. "And you must be Hope." She took Hope's hands in hers, squeezing gently. "Welcome to Lone Oaks."

"Thank you, Mrs. Blackwood. I appreciate you having me."

"Please call me Anna," she insisted.

Because she couldn't help herself, Hope returned Anna's

smile and nodded. "Yes, ma'am." Drew had been right. She hadn't been here ten minutes, and already his mother had made her feel welcome with no more than a smile.

Somewhere in her mid to late fifties, Anna Blackwood could easily have passed for a woman ten years younger. Although by no means overweight, she was full-figured with a short cap of dark hair liberally threaded with silver, and laugh lines fanning out from the corners of her beautiful chocolate brown eyes.

"I'm Zach," the boy who opened the door piped up. "Alex is helping my dad with the chores at the barn."

Hope extended her hand. "It's very nice to meet you, Zach," she returned as they shook. He was a handsome little guy with a face like an angel and devilish blue eyes nearly identical to his uncle's. "I'm Hope."

"Where's Gramps?" Drew asked Zach.

"With Dad and Alex. I wanted to go, too, but they said I needed to stay here with Gram," he lamented in the way only a put-upon five-year-old can.

"Be glad you were assigned indoor duty. It's getting pretty cold out there."

"I like the cold."

"Of course you do. But if you were outside right now, I wouldn't get to do this." Drew hefted Zach, turning him upside down and tickling him mercilessly.

In between fits of giggles, Zach pleaded halfheartedly for Drew to stop.

"Okay. Okay," Anna intervened after a few more squeals. A smile of pure delight spread across her face as well as her grandson's. "C'mon into the family room."

Drew tossed Zach over his shoulder like a sack of potatoes and followed his mother, then he unceremoniously dumped the boy onto the smaller of the two leather sofas.

"Are you hungry?" Anna asked, her gaze darting between

Drew and Hope. "I've got some homemade bread and leftover roast beef. I could make you a sandwich."

"Thank you, but we ate not too long ago," Hope answered, glancing at Drew, who nodded his agreement.

"Well, at least let me get you both something to drink. Tea okay?"

"Water is fine for me, thanks," Hope replied.

With a nod, Anna turned her attention to Drew. "How about you?"

"Tea's good. But I can get it."

"Don't be silly. Take off your coats and get comfortable. I'll be right back."

Once they were rid of their jackets and he'd tossed them over the parson's bench in the foyer, Drew and Hope sat on the sectional sofa facing the fire. About a foot separated them. "You okay?" Drew asked, his voice low.

Hope nodded. "You were right," she whispered. "Your mom is very welcoming."

"Told you."

"Don't rub it in."

He flashed her a grin that had Hope's stomach plunging to her knees. "Hopefully, her reception eased your worries some."

It did. The last thing Hope wanted was to be a burden. She knew it was still early in her visit, and she'd only met his mother and nephew, but her anxieties had lessened significantly.

Of course, having Drew nearby didn't hurt anything either.

Anna returned with their drinks. "The truck just pulled up, so the evening chores must be finished."

"Yippee!" Zach squealed as he hopped off the couch. "I'm gonna tell Dad and Alex that it's my turn to help with the chores tomorrow."

Before he could zip past his grandmother, Anna held out an arm, pulling him up short against her legs. "Let your daddy get in the door before you assault him."

"Oh, Gram."

Within thirty seconds, two men about the same height and build, along with a pint-sized version, walked into the large country kitchen that overlooked the great room. They hadn't gotten three steps in before Zach wiggled free of his grandmother's hold and hurtled toward them. "Uncle Drew's here!"

A smile eased into Drew's lightly stubbled cheeks as he stood to greet his father, brother, and oldest nephew.

"I was hoping that was your truck out there," the older of the two men said as he clasped Drew's hand, pulling him in for a one-armed hug and a hearty pat on the back. "Otherwise, I might have had to sedate your Mama. She was up before dawn waiting for you to get here," he teased with a wink in Anna's direction.

"If my memory serves, you were up pretty early yourself, Eli Blackwood," Anna countered, clearly not about to be bested by her husband.

His blue eyes—the same piercing blue as Drew's—twinkled playfully. "I'm up early every morning, darlin'," he reminded her.

"Not *that* early," Anna pointed out, her dark eyes sparkling with a glimmer of their own.

"Well, I'm sure this young lady here isn't interested in what time we all got up this morning."

"That's Uncle Drew's girlfriend," Zach announced before his grandfather had a chance to introduce himself. "Her name's Hope."

It was the second time in less than ten minutes Zach had referred to Hope as "Uncle Drew's girlfriend." Although the innocent perception of a five-year-old, the inaccuracy of the description still made Hope uncomfortable, and she wondered when Drew would set the record straight with his family.

"Hello, Hope. I'm Eli, Drew's father." Eli Blackwood's large work-calloused hand swallowed Hope's smaller one in a hearty shake. "It's a pleasure to meet you," he added with a smile that warmed his eyes by several degrees.

"Same here," Hope replied, her gaze encompassing Drew's parents. "I really appreciate you opening your home to me on such short notice. I hope I'm not causing you any trouble."

"Not at all." Eli squeezed her hand before releasing it. "We're happy to have you."

"That's right," Anna agreed, stepping up beside her husband.

"Are you a horse doctor like Uncle Drew?" the older of Drew's nephews asked as he shouldered his way between the adults and his little brother.

Hope nodded. "I sure am." Her gaze lowered to meet another pair of those dazzling blue eyes she decided to describe as Blackwood blues, since everyone but Anna seemed to have them. "We work together in Kentucky."

"With horses?"

"Every day."

"We have horses here."

"Millions," Zach added.

"Shut up, doofus," Alex shot back. "Nobody has millions of horses."

"You shut up," Zach countered.

"She was talking to me, anyhow," Alex pointed out.

"She didn't say your name."

"Doesn't matter. She was looking at me."

"I can still answer if I want to."

"Boys," a deep voice from behind them spoke, the tone a clear warning. "That's enough." The order brooked no argument, and even though Alex and Zach still gave each other blistering looks, neither said another word.

Though the man had come in with Eli and Alex, he hung back during the welcoming and introduction period. Not wanting to join in, it appeared, until the boys started neglecting their manners and forced his hand.

"Hope, this is Reese, the father of these hooligans and Drew's older brother," Anna performed the introductions.

He inclined his dark head toward her. "Nice to meet you."

"Same here."

Reese Blackwood was a couple of inches taller than both his brother and his father. His hair was walnut brown, the ends curling into the collar of his flannel blue and gray plaid work shirt, and his square jaw sported what appeared to be a couple days' growth of beard. Although handsome like his brother, his features were drawn, almost flat, his mouth a thin, hard line.

Despite his hooded gaze, Hope saw he bore the same blue eyes as Drew and their father, the same piercing blue he'd obviously passed on to his own sons, only in Reese's, there was no brightness. No devilment lurking in their depths. Only a deep and haunting sadness.

Hope's heart broke for him.

"Sorry about their display of poor manners," Reese added with a nod toward his sons.

"Yeah, sorry," both boys muttered, their eyes lifting to their father's.

"No worries," Hope assured them. "Maybe you can show me your horses while I'm here."

Both their features lit up like miniature Christmas trees. "Maybe we could go riding one day," Alex suggested, his eyes dancing with excitement before his gaze narrowed as a thought occurred to him. "You do know how to ride, don't you?"

Considering she'd likely been on the back of a horse before taking her first steps, Hope suppressed a laugh. "Yeah, I know how to ride," she assured him.

Before any further discussion continued on the subject of horses, the back door opened, ushering in a gust of cold air and a slender older woman with soft green eyes and stylishly coiffed white hair. On her heels followed a tall, strapping man with a thick silver mane and the same stunning blue eyes as every male in the room.

"Thought someone was supposed to call us old folks when Uncle Drew got here," the giant man stated, his voice a booming baritone as his eyes settled on the youngest of his great-grandsons.

"Oops," Zach gulped. "Sorry, Pops."

Chuckling, the older man ruffled the boy's hair. "Guess we'll forgive you this time. Right, Grandma?"

"I suppose," she replied with a smile in her eyes. Then her gaze lifted to the grandson whose arrival Zach had neglected to announce. "Drew." Her smile widened, and her arms opened wide.

Without hesitation, Drew pulled his grandmother in for a big hug. "Hello, beautiful," he greeted, dropping a kiss on her powdery cheek.

"She's not the only one here, boy."

Laughing, Drew stepped back but kept his arm around his grandmother's thin shoulders. "Pops."

The older man enveloped Drew's outstretched hand. "Glad you're here, Andrew."

"Me too," Drew replied, turning toward Hope. "Grandma, Pops, this is Hope Logan. Hope, my grandmother, Sarah Blackwood, and my grandfather, Zeke."

"It's a pleasure to meet you, Dr. and Mrs. Blackwood." Smiling, Hope extended her hand, but instead of taking it, Zeke pulled her in for a bone-crushing bear hug.

"We're not much on formality around here, girlie. Just call me Pops or Doc." He nodded toward his wife. "And the light of my life here can be Gran, Grandma, or Sarah."

With a smile that crinkled the corners of her lovely eyes, Sarah squeezed Hope's hand. "That's right."

For the next hour or so, they all sat around the family room, catching up as the rest of Drew's family trickled in. Holden was first, then Jack and a woman he introduced as his best friend, Tess. Once everyone was in attendance, they all enjoyed a slice of Anna's homemade apple pie topped with a generous scoop of vanilla ice cream.

Quietly, Hope sat back and observed the Blackwood reunion. Despite everyone but Drew living in Beaumont, she gleaned from their conversation it was still difficult to ever have everyone under the same roof at the same time. Hope could also tell by the smile that hadn't left Anna's face since they'd arrived how delighted she was to have all four of her boys within hugging distance.

It tugged at Hope's heart. She thought about the baby she carried. Another branch on the Blackwood family tree to be welcomed and loved by everyone in this room.

By nine o'clock, they all appeared to feel the effects of the long day. Most had been up well before dawn, either busy with traveling, manual farm labor, or any of the other bazillion things to do on a working horse and cattle farm.

"Well, I don't know about the rest of you, but I'm beat," Drew declared, his attention shifting to his mother. "Where do you want me to put our things, Mama?"

Zeke leaped to his feet. For a big man, he moved with the grace of a cat. "You're gonna be staying with us," he informed them.

Smiling, Sarah nodded. "We have the basement apartment all ready for you." She looked at Hope. "It's got a kitchen, dining area, living room, and a bedroom suite with a full bath."

Though Hope wondered what a *bedroom suite* included since the keyword *bedroom* was singular, she had to admit the rest of the living space sounded perfect.

"Since you'll be making the rounds with me while you're here, it only made sense for you to stay with us. Plus, it'll give you some privacy as well," Zeke explained with a devilish wink. "I'm sure you don't want to spend every waking moment with this motley crew."

As expected, Drew's family had already concluded they

were much more than friends. Or coworkers. Hope knew they should set the record straight sooner rather than later, but she just wasn't up to braving those waters tonight. Especially not in the presence of Drew's entire family.

No. Right now, all Hope wanted was a hot shower and about twelve hours of uninterrupted sleep. Everything else could wait a bit longer.

CHAPTER SIX

"Nice house," Hope observed when Drew pulled into the driveway encircling his grandparents' house.

Silver Oaks was a rambling log and stone rancher with a gabled roof, a wealth of windows, and a covered porch stretching across the front. "It's more than they need, but aside from the main house, it's the only home they've shared since they've been married."

They stepped out of the truck, and Zeke tossed Drew a set of keys. Everyone made their way into the apartment, either pulling or carrying the luggage they'd unloaded from the truck. Once they deposited their belongings on the kitchen's knotty pine floor, Zeke gave them the nickel tour, more for Hope's benefit since Drew and his brothers has spent many a night in the basement during sleepovers with their grandparents.

The apartment had hardwood floors and white painted walls. The kitchen was separated from the living area by a raised wooden breakfast bar with stools lining one side and a granite workspace on the other. An L-shaped kitchen with stainless steel appliances, gray-speckled countertops, and glass-fronted pine cabinetry lay behind the island.

An eating area was nestled in the right corner of the kitchen and melded into the living room, where a chocolate microfiber sofa flanked by two matching recliners faced an entertainment center built around a river rock fireplace. A narrow curving staircase led to the main level, and the closed door on the right opened into a bedroom suite complete with a king-sized bed covered in a blue and white handmade quilt. A large mirrored oak dresser faced the bed with matching nightstands on each side.

"We've stocked the fridge, freezer, and pantry with everything we thought you'd need to start with, at least," Sarah informed them, opening a few cabinet doors for confirmation. "Feel free to come upstairs to visit with us whenever you want. I fix plenty to eat, so don't worry there won't be enough. Breakfast is around seven, lunch by noon, and supper at six."

"Thank you so much, but I wish you hadn't gone to so much trouble," Hope replied.

"No trouble at all," his grandfather assured her. "Since I know you're plumb worn out from the drive, we'll let you two get settled." He motioned his wife toward the stairs. "We'll be sure to knock before coming down," Zeke promised with a wink as he hustled Sarah up the steps.

Hope stood in the middle of the living room. Her shoulders sagged, and smudges darkened the skin beneath her eyes. Traveling six hundred miles in one day was enough to wear anyone out. But add in Hope's anxiety levels about meeting his family, the continued grief she still suffered from losing her father, and the fact that she was four months pregnant, it was no wonder she appeared on the verge of collapse.

"C'mon." Drew took Hope's hand and led her straight through the bedroom to the en suite bathroom. He turned on the water in the glass-enclosed shower and pulled two large fluffy green towels and a washcloth from the linen closet. "I'll get your bags."

Hope raised her eyes to meet his, and the exhaustion he saw reflected in the amber depths slayed him. "You don't have to wait on me, Drew."

The hell he didn't. "I know. But you're completely worn out."

"And you're not?"

Reaching out, Drew tucked an errant strand of hair behind her ear, his fingers lingering along the soft skin of her jaw. "I'm not tied up in knots the way you are." He cupped her cheek in his palm. "And I'm not carrying a baby."

Hope's hooded gaze locked on his. "I don't have the energy to argue about it."

"Good." Drew smiled. "Now, go on and get your shower."

———

Nearly forty minutes passed before Hope emerged from the bathroom. She'd stood under the pulsing jets for a good ten minutes, letting the water pound against her aching muscles. Who knew just riding in a truck for twelve hours could be so draining? And take such a toll on the body?

After wiggling into a pair of nondescript white cotton panties, Hope pulled on a thigh-length navy blue tee that doubled as a nightgown and slipped into an oversized turquoise fleece robe that tied at her waist and fell to her ankles.

With her hair in a haphazard top knot, Hope padded into the living room and found Drew seated in one of the recliners, flipping through the channels on the flat-screen TV. He'd set her a glass of milk on the end table by the sofa.

"Hey." Hope moved a crimson throw pillow and eased onto the nut-brown sofa.

"Hey, yourself." Drew dialed down the volume on the TV and motioned toward the glass of milk with the remote. "I figured since you can't have beer or wine, I couldn't go wrong with milk. I can warm it up if you'd like."

"No. This is fine. Thank you." Hope took a generous gulp and wiped her lips with the sleeve of her robe. "I'm trying to limit my caffeine intake to one cup of coffee per day, and I've switched to green tea since it's decaffeinated and full of antioxidants."

"Lots of changes, huh?"

Hope shrugged. "Healthy ones, at least." She took another drink. "I enjoyed meeting your family."

He swiveled the recliner toward her. "The feeling was mutual."

"Your nephews are adorable."

Drew smiled. "Yeah. Ornery as hell but adorable."

"Probably much like you and your brothers were at their age."

"I'm sure my mother would tell you we were much worse."

Tucking her feet beneath her, Hope set the glass on the table. "I can't get over all those blue eyes."

"Except for Jack and Mama. They inherited their brown eyes from Mama's side of the family—the Beauregards."

"So, Blackwood blues and Beauregard browns, huh?"

Drew chuckled, causing tiny lines to fan out from the corners of his very own Blackwood blues. "I never thought about it like that, but I guess so."

Hope wondered what color eyes their baby would inherit.

Wow! What a totally unexpected thought. Before she began to hyperventilate on the matter, Hope changed the subject. "Your mother is glad to have you home."

His brow knitted together. "Why do you say that?"

"The smile never left her face, and she couldn't take her eyes off you."

He rolled his own eyes. "If you say so."

"You know damn well she's happy you're here."

A slow grin eased into his cheeks. "Yeah. I know."

Of course he did. "Well, thanks to Zach, I know Lone Oaks has *millions* of horses. What other kinds of animals live here?"

"The exaggerations of a five-year-old." Drew shook his head. "Let's see, there's about twenty-five hundred head of Black Angus, a few hogs, some chickens, and who knows how many barn cats."

"And a wolf," Hope added, referring to the huge blue-eyed silvery gray dog that greeted them upon their arrival.

"Only half," Drew clarified. "But you'll never find a more loyal pet than Sadie."

"Or a more intimidating one. I bet not too many strangers amble onto your property with her around."

"Initially, she does present quite the fear factor. Yet while I have no doubt she'd die protecting any one of us, she's really just a big ol' sweetheart. Especially if you're giving her any attention."

Yeah, Hope had noticed how Sadie's eyes rolled back in her head while Drew lovingly rubbed the sweet spot behind her ears. Hope could relate. She felt the same light-headed delirium whenever Drew touched her.

Dang. Where did *that* thought come from? They were talking about the animals at Lone Oaks. How did that segue into how Drew's touch made her feel?

Maybe because right now, you'd like nothing more than to have his hands all over you.

Or maybe my hormones are just running amok, Hope silently challenged the nagging little voice in her head.

Still, though she might prefer to deny it, Hope *was* attracted to Drew. Had been from the first day they'd met. And why wouldn't she be? Drew was every woman's dream, with his compelling lake-blue eyes, mouth-watering hard-bodied physique, and downright lethal smile. Hell, even the scar bisecting his right eyebrow tangled her panties in a knot.

Hope would need to be comatose for Drew to have no

effect on her at all. Even then, she'd probably still sense his presence. He had that potent an effect on her.

And likely most every other female he encountered.

"Since Pops will likely want to get started in the morning at the butt crack of dawn, we'd better get some sleep," Drew interrupted Hope's thoughts.

"You make him sound terrible."

"Not terrible. Relentless." He sat forward in the recliner. "Like a dog with a bone. Especially when he has his mind set on something." He smiled knowingly. "You'll see."

"He just wants you to stay. To have his family all in one place." As the words left her lips, Hope felt the knife slice through her heart at the reminder he could very well decide not to return to Kentucky.

"That's his number one priority for sure."

"Can you blame him?"

Drew's gaze locked on hers. The dimness in the room darkened his eyes. "No, I guess not." He rose from the chair. "But that won't make his campaign any less exhausting." Turning, Drew carried his empty glass to the sink, rinsed it out, and stuck it in the dishwasher.

"Since you probably want to shower, I'll just curl up here on the sofa for the night."

"No," Drew replied and closed the dishwasher. "You get the bed."

Hope looked from Drew to the couch. There was no way in hell he would get any kind of rest trying to fit his six-foot-plus frame on the raised-arm, three-cushion sofa. She doubted the recliners would be much better. "That's ridiculous."

"What? For you to sleep in a bed?"

"No, dumb ass. For *you* to sleep on the couch."

"But I'm not pregnant."

"And I didn't spend twelve hours driving across two states. Nor am I twice the length of that sofa."

"But..."

Hope raised her palm toward him, stopping him from saying anything more. "I appreciate you being a gentleman, Drew, but do you really think I'll get a wink of sleep knowing how cramped up you'll be on this couch?"

"And you think I'll sleep any better with you out here?"

Lord, they were a hot mess.

Then, it hit her. "We do have one other option."

"We do?" Skeptically, he narrowed his gaze.

"Yeah." Hope nodded. "I'm sure that king-sized bed in there is plenty big enough for us both to be comfortable and get a much-needed good night's sleep."

He arched a dark brow. "You sure about that?"

"About what? That the bed is big enough for us both to be comfortable, or that we'll get a good night's sleep?"

"Either." Drew cocked his head to the side. "Or both."

Hope shrugged. "I'm already pregnant, Drew. For us to sleep separately would be like closing the barn door after the horse already got out, don't you think?"

The furrow deepened between his brows, indicating he wasn't sure he agreed with her logic. "You need to be absolutely sure, because there's no guarantee we won't accidentally touch in the night. So, if that's going to be a problem, I better sleep out here."

"It won't be a problem," she assured him.

"You're sure?"

Too tired to argue further, Hope sighed and headed for the bedroom. "Turn out the lights."

By the time Drew emerged from the bathroom, Hope was snuggled under the covers on the left side of the California king. "Want me to leave the light on and crack the door a little in case you have to get up in the night?"

"I'll be fine. Thanks."

She heard him snap off the light and toss his clothes into

the suitcase. When he eased onto the other side of the bed, a nervous flutter skittered through Hope's belly. From his movements and the dip in the mattress, Hope could tell Drew was lying on his back and had pulled the sheet and blanket up to his waist.

Though they were nowhere close to touching, the heat radiating off Drew's big body still sent a shiver clear to her toes. Maybe sharing a bed, even as big as this one, wasn't such a bright idea. Sure, it was physically more comfortable, but with her nerves strung so tight she could have played a tune, Hope doubted any valuable shuteye was in her immediate future.

Maybe if they talked a little, it would help her relax.

"How long was Reese married before his wife passed away?" It might not have been the best topic, but it was a thousand times better than the radio silence stretching awkwardly between them.

"About eight years."

"I can't imagine how hard it has to be for him. First, to lose his wife, then trying to raise two small boys while running a horse and cattle farm the size of Lone Oaks."

"Both the farm and the boys are what keep him functioning at all. He can't even live in the house he built for himself and Olivia. That's why he and the boys stay at the main house with our parents."

"Grief can be a bitch." Hope could attest to that, and her heart ached for Reese and his boys. "Losing anyone is devastating, but someone in the prime of their life? I don't know how you'd get over something like that."

"Me neither." The sheets rustled as he shifted slightly. "I'm sure Pops will expect me to go with him on some calls tomorrow," Drew deftly changed the subject. "You're welcome to come along if you want, but I don't want you to feel obligated if you aren't up to it."

"I'd like to tag along if you don't think your grandfather will mind." It'd be interesting to see the kind of work the elder veterinarian's practice entailed. And to also see a little bit of where Drew had been born and raised.

"He'll love it," Drew answered. "But if you're too tired..."

"I'd be working if I was back home," Hope reminded him, halting his need to stipulate.

"But you wouldn't have just ridden six hundred miles in one day either."

Hope rolled onto her back. "You're not going to spend the next five months worrying about everything I do, are you?"

Drew turned his head on the pillow to look at her. "Probably."

"Well, please don't."

He turned on his side to face her. The covers settled around his waist, leaving his torso bare. Skin still tan from the summer sun stretched across the muscles of his chest and abdomen. God, he was a beautiful man.

"In fact, since I have no firsthand knowledge when it comes to human pregnancies, I'm likely to be overly cautious and question everything." Reaching out, he brushed the back of his forefinger against her cheek. "You're going to have to be patient with me, okay?"

Hope's heart swelled, turning her insides to mush. "I'm not going to do anything I shouldn't do."

"Do you regret it?" Drew asked quietly, the weight of his gaze on her face.

Hope wasn't sure if he meant the pregnancy or the night they'd slept together. Not that it mattered, because if she hadn't invited him into her bed, she also wouldn't be pregnant with his child. Either way, there was no simple answer.

"Conflicted is probably a more apt description than regret."

"About?"

"Everything." At this point, the better question was more likely what wasn't conflicting her. "Being pregnant. Am I doing what I should for the baby? Am I mother material? Or rather, will I be like my own mother and wake up one morning to decide I don't want to be a parent anymore? And if I'm fortunate enough not to inherit her walk-away-and-never-look-back gene, will I be able to manage a veterinary career as a single parent?"

"You're not going to be a single parent, Hope. I'm going to be with you every step of the way."

Unless you decide to stay here, Hope thought but didn't dare say out loud. "I know," she replied instead.

"But?"

"But I'm sure this isn't exactly how you planned on becoming a father. You have to be as conflicted, scared, apprehensive, and overwhelmed as I am."

"Yeah. I am. But there is one thing I am one hundred percent sure about." He traced the edge of her jaw with his thumb. "Regardless of how this baby was conceived, there is no one I'd rather have as the mother of my child than you."

Hope's heart shifted inside her chest. Almost as if things were falling into place.

At six-thirty the following morning, Hope found Drew at the kitchen table, finishing what she guessed was his first caffeine infusion. "Good morning," she greeted him as she opened a few cabinets in search of a mug.

"Mornin'. I tried to be quiet so I wouldn't wake you."

Hope shook her head. "Internal alarm clock." She popped a pod in the Keurig. As the coffee began its drip, Hope noticed Drew was dressed in his customary attire of faded jeans, work boots, and long-sleeved henley, which today was hunter green. "Have you eaten?"

"You don't have to cook for me."

"I know I don't, but if I'm gonna fix myself something, it's just as easy to make enough for both of us." Hope opened the fridge, pulled out a carton of eggs and a slab of bacon. "Have you heard from your grandfather?" She cracked several eggs into a bowl and whisked them together with a dash of salt, pepper, and milk.

"No. Which is surprising." Drew rose to brew himself another cup of coffee, and his clean manly scent enveloped Hope, knocking her for a loop.

Damn hormones.

"I thought he'd either be down here or have called by now." Drew turned toward her. "Need any help?"

Hope laid the strips of bacon side by side in the cast iron skillet and adjusted the flame to medium. "Um, bread for toast?"

While Hope grabbed another skillet, sprayed it with cooking oil, and poured the eggs into it, Drew pulled out a loaf of bread from a metal-lined drawer. For the next ten minutes, they worked in companionable silence. Drew dropped the bread into the toaster, buttered it when it popped back up, and Hope monitored the stove until the eggs were fluffy, the bacon crisp.

They'd just tucked into their meal when a loud pounding on the door at the top of the stairs startled them both. "Okay to come down?" Zeke bellowed.

"Yeah," Drew yelled back.

Pops descended the steps. "I smelled bacon frying, so I figured somebody was up."

"Good morning, Doc."

"And a fine morning it is." A twinkle danced in his Blackwood blues as he snatched a piece of bacon from Drew's plate. "Sure is good to have all my grandsons back on Lone Oaks soil. Just the way the good Lord intended."

With an arched brow, Drew looked at Hope over the rim

of his coffee mug as if to say, *See, I told you*, regarding the old man's ploy to pull out every stop in his crusade to convince Drew that Virginia was where he belonged.

Though it didn't make anything easier in her world, Hope couldn't blame Zeke's tenacity. If she had family, she'd want them nearby as well.

"Can I get you some breakfast, Doc?"

"No, thanks. Miss Sarah sent me off with a full belly, as usual, this morning." He patted the stomach area of his bib overalls for emphasis.

"Are you on your way out on a call?" Drew asked as Hope took their dishes to the sink.

"You comin' along if I am?"

"That was the plan for me coming home, wasn't it?"

Zeke's massive shoulders lifted and fell in a shrug. "Didn't know if you were planning to start right away. Thought you might want a couple days to settle in, get your bearings, and show your girl around a bit first. I figured starting the Monday after Thanksgiving would be soon enough."

"You sure?"

"Yep. Besides, I'm only going to the clinic this morning," Zeke clarified.

According to Drew, in addition to the various farms in the area he serviced, Doc also owned and operated Lone Oaks Animal Care, where he treated smaller animals by appointment a few days a week. "But I'm sure your grandmother would be over the moon to have you both join her for lunch."

Drew nodded. "We'll plan on it."

"Hope, it certainly is a pleasure to have you here."

She smiled as she dried the skillet. "Thanks, Doc. It's nice to be here." And it was.

"At least one of you thinks so," he muttered before turning and disappearing out the door rather than heading back upstairs.

"That was an unexpected surprise," Drew admitted before draining his coffee mug.

Hope wiped off the stove and countertops. "He doesn't seem like an unreasonable man, Drew." She swiped the dishcloth over the table. "I'm sure he understands about our long drive yesterday. And since it's been a while since you've been back, he's probably just allowing you a chance to settle and get your bearings before diving into the deep end. Plus, Thanksgiving is in two days."

"Yeah. You're right." He didn't sound convinced.

"Are you sorry you agreed to come?" Hope crossed her arms and leaned a jean-clad hip against the counter.

"Not yet."

"Your entire family is glad to have you home, Drew. For however long or short the visit."

"But what happens if, after this six-week trial run, I decide to stay at Wakefield?"

"Plan more visits?"

Drew plowed his fingers through his thick hair. "That's one option, I guess."

"Yeah, it is."

"They'll still be disappointed."

"But they'll understand." Hope pushed herself away from the counter and narrowed the gap between them. "Because regardless of where you choose to continue practicing, all they truly want is for you to be happy."

"You really think so?"

"I'm positive."

"I'm gonna hold you to that," Drew forewarned her with a smile.

Rising, he took his mug to the sink and rinsed it out before stashing it on the top rack in the dishwasher. "Since we don't have to play veterinarian today, how about I give you a tour of Beaumont?"

"Will we still be able to have lunch with your grandmother?"

"It's not exactly a booming metropolis." Drew grinned, and Hope's heart stuttered. "I think we'll be back in plenty of time."

"I'll get my coat."

CHAPTER SEVEN

By Thanksgiving, Hope and Drew had been in Virginia two full days. On Tuesday, after breakfast, Drew showed Hope around Lone Oaks as well as Beaumont proper, the epitome of small-town America. There were no shopping or strip malls, big-box department stores, or fast-food franchises; only quaint shops, locally owned eating establishments, and family-run businesses.

With its one stoplight, an abundance of foot traffic, and absence of public transportation, Beaumont was quite different from where Hope grew up in Kentucky, but as she and Drew strolled down Main Street, Hope instantly fell in love with the welcoming appeal of the humble little burg.

Though only three and a half blocks long, Hope could easily spend days exploring the vast array of privately owned establishments, each with its own unique wide-windowed storefront shaded by awnings, porticoes, or strategically placed flowering dogwoods. She yearned to wander aimlessly from shop to shop, discovering every single one of their treasures, indulging in everything each had to offer.

She especially wanted to check out Serendipity, the gift shop that included just a little bit of everything; the Artisan's and Grower's Market, which sold locally sourced food, a wide array of handcrafted wares, and a large section of art in various mediums—all of which was grown or crafted by local farmers and artisans; and Sugar Whipped, the bakery that offered everything that smelled delicious and no doubt tasted even better.

After Drew promised to bring her back for a more thorough exploration of Beaumont as well as Sheridan, they returned to Lone Oaks for a lovely lunch with his grandmother. Sarah Blackwood was as petite as her husband was strapping, but Hope had no doubt the tiny woman with her sharp green eyes could be as strong-willed as any of the men in her family.

Probably even more.

It was also evident by her perpetual smile that she was beyond ecstatic to have her second-oldest grandson home.

Once they'd finished with lunch, they'd gone to the main house, where Hope had visited with Drew's mother, assisting her with dinner preparations while Drew went out to help his father and Reese with the endless chores on a farm the size of Lone Oaks.

The next day, after assuring Drew she and the baby would be fine, they'd gone riding, helped separate cattle to be culled, enjoyed lunch at one of the family-run diners in town, and visited a few of the locally owned shops. After dinner with Jack, Tess and Holden, they'd returned to the basement apartment to catch up on email and watch a little TV before heading to bed.

Except for the afternoon he'd left Hope with his mother, Drew had never been far from her side. Hope appreciated that he hadn't left her to fend for herself. Still, her overactive hormones combined with Drew's round-the-clock nearness amplified her attraction to him a thousand-fold, making her want to do so much more with him than simply share a bed where all they did was sleep.

And that was only after two days and three nights in Virginia. How in the world was she ever going to survive thirty more?

Groaning inwardly, Hope rolled over and nuzzled Drew's pillow, inhaling his spicy scent as she listened to the hum of the shower on the other side of the bathroom door. Though she'd slept more soundly with Drew beside her than she had in previous weeks, the sexual tension intensified, winding her tighter than an eight-day clock.

Like now, for instance, when all Hope wanted to do was strip naked and join him in the shower. Explore every inch of his gloriously delicious body. Tasting and touching until she drove him as crazy as living in his pocket was driving her.

If she weren't careful, Hope was bound to find herself in another impossible situation. One where she fell head over heels for her baby daddy only to have her heart ripped to shreds when he came to the realization Lone Oaks was where he belonged. With his family. Joining his grandfather's practice.

Returning home.

Hope's heart ached as she imagined what life at Wakefield would be like without him.

Damn you, Sam Logan. If you were still on this earth, I wouldn't be so far away from home, pregnant with my boss's baby, and lusting after him like some under-sexed hormonal teenager. Instead, I'd be home where I belong, having Thanksgiving dinner with you and whoever you decided to invite to our table.

But Sam was gone. And here she was. In Virginia. With Drew. And Hope wasn't sure, if given a choice, she'd want to be anywhere else.

Damn! What the hell was happening to her?

Okay, first, Hope realized there was no point denying she was and had been in deep lust with Drew since he arrived at Wakefield. And seriously, what red-blooded woman wouldn't be? The man was a freaking work of art. But until hopping into his pickup on Monday morning for the long-ass drive to Virginia, her fixation with him hadn't been so...intense.

Three days ago, the spicy scent of his aftershave hadn't intoxicated her as if it were smooth Kentucky bourbon. Her breath hadn't caught in her throat every time he walked into the room. And her girlie parts hadn't exploded at the way the fabric of his shirt and jeans clung to the rock-hard muscles of his arms, torso, and thighs.

Now though, his eyes seemed bluer. His smile warmer. His ass tighter. How in the hell was she going to last the weekend with Drew, let alone another whole month, without spontaneously combusting?

When she heard the buzz of Drew's electric razor, Hope pictured him with nothing more than a towel tied loosely around his lean waist as he stood before the steamed-up mirror above the sink and ran the razor over his chiseled jaw. Was there anything sexier than a man shaving? At the moment, she didn't think so.

Groaning, Hope rolled back onto her side of the bed, an ache as old as time throbbing through her core.

Ten minutes and a thousand deep breaths later, Drew emerged from the bathroom, his smile quick and warm. "Mornin', sunshine."

Hope's stomach dove straight to her toes. God, she'd never wanted another man more in her life. "Mornin'," she managed to reply without coming apart at the seams. Just looking at him, so big and delicious, warmed her from the inside out.

It wasn't like he looked any different today than any other day she'd seen him. He'd pulled on faded boot-cut jeans and was buttoning a blue chambray shirt as he kicked his well-worn leather boots to his side of the bed. Nothing fancy. Nothing out of the ordinary. Certainly, nothing to make her want to climb him like a tree.

Yet, the moment he sat on the bed to slip his feet into a pair of socks, it took every ounce of willpower Hope had not to strip naked and devour him. That was when she realized she could no longer blame her fierce reaction to Drew on pregnancy hormones alone. Everything she felt for him was too deep. Too elemental.

Too freaking real.

In what would likely be a futile attempt to gain some control over the desire raging through her entire body, Hope sucked in a deep breath and pushed herself to a sitting position on the bed. "You're up kind of early for a holiday." At least her voice didn't sound like belonging to the sexually frustrated woman she'd become.

"I thought I'd give Dad and Reese a hand this morning so all that'll need to be done later is the evening feeding."

"Want me to fix you some breakfast before you go?" Maybe channeling her energies elsewhere would help.

Drew shook his still damp head. "Nah. I'm good." He bent to tie his boots.

"Is there anything I can do?" Like strip you naked and ride you like a Harley on a bad piece of road?

"Maybe if you're up to it, you can check with Mama and see if she could use an extra pair of hands." He moved to the other boot. "I'll leave the truck here so you can drive up when you're ready."

All things considered, that was probably a better alternative than jumping his bones.

For now, anyway. "How will *you* get to the farm?" The main house, barns, and livestock areas were all a good mile away.

Straightening, he looked over his shoulder at her. "Reese is on his way to pick me up."

"Oh." Spending the morning with Drew's mother should cool her off a bit. "Then I'll get ready and head to the main house."

His lips curved into a smile that slashed into his clean-shaven cheeks. Hope's heart skipped a beat. Or ten. "I'm sure Mama'll appreciate it." A horn beeped. "There's Reese."

Drew pushed off the bed and grabbed his jacket. "See ya later."

"Drew?"

"Yeah?"

"What should I wear? I mean, is there an expectation of how to dress? Thanksgiving with Sam was always informal, but I don't want to assume everyone has the same casual dress code we did." Yes, think about clothes. Putting them on for Thanksgiving. With his family.

"Anything is fine," Drew assured her. "We aren't much on formality either. Just be comfortable."

"Okay," Hope replied even though she was no clearer on what to wear now than she'd been before.

When Drew got to the bedroom door, he stopped and turned back toward her. "My mother usually wears something like khakis or black pants. Nothing fancy."

Appreciating how he'd obviously realized she didn't want to wear something that would make her stick out like a sore thumb, Hope smiled. "I can handle that." Finally, something she could control.

———

When Drew and Reese arrived at the barn, they were met by their father, Jack, and Holden. Since the farmhands had been given the day off to spend with their families, the five of them split up the duties. It was quickly decided Reese and Eli would haul round bales out to the fields for the cattle, and Drew, Jack, and Holden would feed and water the horses and muck out the stalls in the main stable.

Jack went outside to tend the horses in the corrals, and Drew and Holden took care of the ones who'd been bedded down in the stable for the night. Although it had been years since the three of them had been involved in the day-to-day operation at Lone Oaks, they fell back into an easy rhythm reminiscent of their younger days spent working alongside their father where it was expected they would all equally pull their weight.

Despite his love of horses, Drew hadn't missed the long hours associated with running a farm the size of Lone Oaks. Since two of his three brothers had also chosen careers outside the farming realm, it was a relief to know he hadn't been the only one who'd yearned for something different than running beef cattle and raising thoroughbreds.

Drew had no idea how Reese did it day in and day out. Farming was unforgiving and exhausting work, demanding more than its fair share of a man's time and energy. Even when a job was finished, it either had to be repeated the next day, or something else arose requiring immediate attention.

Since losing Olivia, Drew figured running Lone Oaks had kept Reese sane and served as a much-needed avenue of escape. By working himself to near collapse daily, his brother wouldn't have the energy to remember his loss, but more importantly, he wouldn't have to feel.

Anything.

"Tell me you don't miss this any more than I do," Holden said from the stall across the concrete aisle from him.

Drew forked manure and urine-saturated straw into the wheelbarrow. "I don't miss it at all," he affirmed, turning back to the unsavory task. "But do you think anyone really enjoys it?"

"As much time as Reese spends out here, he must find some kind of special pleasure in shoveling shit."

Leaning on his pitchfork, Drew considered Holden's comment. "Did he spend as much time working the farm before Olivia passed?"

Holden tossed another forkful into the wheelbarrow. "No." He propped his fork against the wall, cut the twine on a bale of straw, and scattered a handful on the clean floor of the stall. "He was busy, but it was more balanced. He did a lot more supervising, leaving the bulk of the manual labor to Boone and the farmhands," he added, referring to the foreman at Lone Oaks, Boone Randall. "Since Olivia's been gone, though..." Holden trailed off, shaking his head.

Drew tossed a chunk of alfalfa in the hay rack. "You think you'll ever feel that way about a woman? The way Reese must have felt for Olivia?"

"I sure as hell hope not." Holden picked up the fork and moved to the next stall. "Especially after bearing witness to how losing her completely gutted Reese." He went back to fetch the wheelbarrow. "I'm fine with the life I have, thank you very much. No strings. No entanglements. Heart still intact." He patted the middle of his chest. "Yeah, I'm good."

Of the four brothers, Holden had always been the most laid back and carefree. Jack had the movie star looks, but Holden, although handsome in his own right, was more roguish. A maverick of sorts. Rarely did he date the same woman for more than a few months. More likely a couple of weeks. Even less if she became too clingy or started demanding more than he was willing to give.

"Wouldn't you like to have someone waiting for you at the end of each day? Someone to share all the important things in life with?"

Holden tossed another forkful of straw into the wheelbarrow. "Bella's waiting for me every day when I get home from work," he answered, referring to his five-year-old golden retriever. "She's always glad to see me, loyal to a fault, and doesn't give me a bunch of crap if I decide to stop off for a few beers or a bite to eat after work. As for sharing the important things in life, she's a damned good listener too. If I have something I feel the need to share with someone other than Bella, well, that's what brothers are for."

"What about a mother for your children?"

A wicked gleam danced in Holden's cobalt eyes. "That can

be easily accomplished almost anywhere, and it doesn't require a lifelong commitment either."

Yeah, Drew had firsthand knowledge about that.

Pulling the hose along, Holden filled the bucket in the stall with water. "What about you, big brother? You got the itch all of a sudden?"

Until a few weeks ago, Drew hadn't really given it much consideration one way or the other. It wasn't like he'd recently been in a committed relationship or anything. And though he'd been attracted to Hope from the jump, his first inclination hadn't been to put a ring on her finger and start a family.

Yeah, he wanted to be with her. In every way possible. Both then and now. But theirs hadn't exactly been a textbook coupling, that was for damn sure.

There'd been no courting rituals. No official dates. When they went out together, they were just two coworkers grabbing a quick bite to eat or sharing a beer after work. Everything had remained strictly platonic until the cumulative effect of emotional overload and too much tequila overruled them both.

As a result, they not only had to figure out how to move forward as friends and coworkers after their one night of unbridled passion but also what to do about the child they'd created as a result. Like Hope's anxiety regarding motherhood, Drew had similar concerns about becoming a father. Not that their readiness mattered much when, in less than five months, they would indeed become parents.

Whether they would share the experience as a couple, well, that was another concern entirely. Though Hope still had qualms, Drew wanted to give it a shot.

"It's crossed my mind," Drew finally answered Holden's question.

"I don't suppose the leggy brunette with the soulful brown eyes you brought home with you has anything to do with this line of thinking, now, does she?"

Just everything.

Here was a chance to share his dilemma with one of his brothers. To get a different perspective. Admit how much he wanted to be with Hope and raise their child together. As a family.

But he couldn't. Not when he'd promised Hope they wouldn't say anything until she was ready. "We're just friends." At least it wasn't a lie.

"Yeah. Okay." Holden rolled his eyes. "You keep telling yourself that."

Drew stopped and narrowed his gaze at his brother. "What's that supposed to mean?"

Holden shook out some straw, spreading it over the floor with his foot and the pitchfork. "Well," he drawled, "I don't remember you ever bringing a woman home for Thanksgiving before. Let alone one who'll be staying through Christmas into New Year's."

"She recently lost her father, who was the only family she had, Holden. She shouldn't be alone for the holidays. Especially the first ones without her dad."

"So, you haul her across two states to spend the holiday season with you and a bunch of strangers?" Holden shook his head. "I'm sure she has friends she's known a lot longer than you who would've taken her under their wing and looked out for her to make sure she didn't spend the entire holiday season grieving."

"What are you getting at?"

Holden hunched his broad shoulders in a shrug. "Sounds to me like *you* might have been the one who didn't want to spend the holidays without her."

"And what if I didn't?" Drew shot back. Holden had always been good at seeing past the bullshit and diving right to the heart of most matters. He'd been that way his whole life.

Asshole.

"It still doesn't mean anything is going on between us."

One dark brow arched. "Well, now, if I remember correctly, the basement apartment where you're currently staying only has one bedroom. And I don't recall you asking for different accommodations for you and *your friend*."

"Shut the fuck up, Holden."

"Aw, it sounds just like old times," Jack observed as he ambled into the stable. "You guys aren't finished in here yet?"

"We would be if Holden had kept his trap shut long enough."

Holden filled a feed bag with oats in one of the stalls. "Hey, you were the one who started waxing poetic about what Reese and Olivia had and how you might have gotten the itch to settle down. All I did was ask if it had anything to do with the dark-haired beauty you brought here from Kentucky."

Jack nodded. "Sounds like a reasonable question."

"You can shut the hell up too."

Jack lifted both his hands, palms out. "Touchy."

"There isn't anything going on between Hope and me." It was the truth.

Almost.

Just because she was pregnant with his child, and while at Lone Oaks they were sharing a bed for sleeping purposes only, it did not constitute a romance. Or even a relationship. And neither did the fact that Hope mattered more to Drew than any other woman ever had.

"Then you shouldn't have any objections if I take her out and show her around while she's here," Holden replied.

White-hot rage exploded through Drew. "I wouldn't advise it," he warned his brother.

As if at a tennis match, Jack's head turned expectantly back in Holden's direction for the next volley.

"But you just said nothing was going on between the two of you."

One dark brow arched, Jack slid his gaze back to Drew.

"I also said she'd recently lost her father. She doesn't need the likes of you playing with her emotions." Drew, better than anyone, knew exactly what could happen when on emotional overload.

A grin dimpled Holden's cheeks and danced wickedly in his eyes. "I see."

"You know, Drew, it's not a crime to be attracted to a beautiful woman," Jack interrupted the parlay. "Just means you're human."

Both Jack and Holden were right. There wasn't any crime in being attracted to Hope, or anything wrong with not wanting to leave her in Kentucky while he came home. Drew could tell himself it was only because she'd be facing her first holidays without her father, but he knew the real reason was that he didn't want to be separated from Hope for six long weeks.

Hell, he didn't want them to be apart at all.

If only he knew how Hope truly felt. About him and whether she wanted to keep the baby. Not knowing was driving him crazy, but with everything between them still so precarious, he didn't want to risk doing or saying anything that might upset her.

Or drive her back to Kentucky before the New Year.

"You're awfully quiet over there," Holden stated, devilment gleaming in his eyes.

"You've made your point, Holden." Drew stabbed another slab of manure and urine-soaked straw and tossed it into the wheelbarrow. "Now shut the hell up so we can get finished before we miss Thanksgiving dinner altogether."

―――――

About an hour after Drew left, Hope made her way to the main house. Since she'd come early to help Drew's mother with meal prep or whatever else needed to be done, she'd dressed in jeans she could barely button and a dark oversized long-sleeved tee. In a tote, she'd packed more appropriate clothing for dinner.

She'd no more than knocked on the front door when it swung open. "Hey, Hope," Zach greeted. He was barefoot and still in his pajamas. "Gram!" he hollered. "It's Uncle Drew's Hope."

Seeing no point, Hope didn't correct him. First, she'd been Uncle Drew's girlfriend, and now she was his Hope. Guess in Zach's five-year-old mind Hope didn't have an identity of her own. Not that it mattered. But she was a bit surprised at how warm and gooey it made her feel inside to be considered Drew's *anything*.

As Hope allowed that realization to take hold, Drew's mother appeared, wiping her hands on a tea towel slung over her left shoulder. "Why'd'ya leave her standing on the porch?" Anna pulled Zach out of the way with a sigh. "Come in, Hope, and try to overlook my grandson's poor manners."

Hope stepped into the foyer. "Drew went with Reese this morning, so I thought I'd come to see if you needed help with anything."

Smiling, Anna closed the door. "That's very nice of you, but you're a guest. I wouldn't feel right putting you to work."

"Why not? I surely don't expect to do nothing while I'm here. Plus, helping will lessen my guilt for imposing on you and your family for the next few weeks."

Anna led the way into the kitchen. "You're no imposition in the least. We're glad to have you."

"I'm glad to be here, but I still plan on pulling my weight, Mrs. Blackwood."

"Okay. As long as you call me Anna. I'd say my mother-in-law is Mrs. Blackwood, but I'm sure she's already insisted you call her Sarah."

Which she had. Smiling, Hope set her tote on the floor beside the breakfast bar and pushed up the sleeves of her shirt past her elbows. "Tell me what needs to be done."

Looking around, Anna's eyes landed on the sink. "You mind peeling potatoes?"

"Not a bit." Crossing to where the bag of spuds sat, Hope located a knife and set to work.

For the next hour and a half, the two of them fell into a comfortable rhythm of working together. While they peeled, diced, chopped, mixed, and stirred, their conversation was light and companionable, allowing them to get to know each other better without an entire houseful of people to interrupt.

By eleven, the turkey was roasting, potatoes boiling and sauerkraut simmering. Mac and cheese, dressing balls, and sweet potatoes were prepped for baking. Raw veggies were cleaned, cut, and arranged on a platter, and yeast rolls continued to rise on the counter.

And that was only what they'd accomplished since Hope's arrival. Most of the desserts—apple, pecan, and cherry pie, strawberry cheesecake, and peach cobbler—as well as several cold salads had been made the day before, and Sarah was bringing country ham, a green bean casserole, and homemade cranberry sauce.

"Until it's time to put things in the oven to bake, I think we've done about all we can for now," Anna declared as she handed Hope the last dish to dry. Letting the water out of the sink, Anna rinsed out the debris, snapped on the garbage disposal, and then wiped her hands on the tea towel she'd left slung over her shoulder. "We make a pretty good team."

Indeed, they did.

"How about some coffee?" Anna asked as she popped a pod in the machine.

"I'd love some." Once she'd gotten up and dressed, Hope hadn't stopped to brew her one allotted cup before coming to help Drew's mother.

They sat down at the oblong walnut table nestled in the breakfast nook. "You have a beautiful home," Hope complimented.

"Thank you." Anna took a sip of her steaming coffee. "We built on the back section after Jack was born and upgraded in a few areas over the years, but for the most part, aside from the décor, it's pretty much the same as when Zeke built it for himself and Sarah."

"It's big but so cozy and warm. Very homey."

"With four boys, it was often a disaster zone." Anna chuckled. "There were days I wasn't sure I'd survive."

"I can't even imagine." The testosterone overload alone would have been impossible to manage, Hope was sure. Especially during the teenage years. That Anna Blackwood only had a smattering of gray threads in her dark hair was admirable.

"Do you have any brothers or sisters?" Anna asked.

Hope shook her head. "No. Well, none that I know about. My mom left when I was five. I have no idea if she ever had any other children."

Sympathy shone in Anna's amber eyes. "I'm so sorry." She laid her hand over Hope's and squeezed.

"It's hard to miss what you never had," Hope replied. "Besides, my father was the absolute best. Always there, no matter what. Present in every moment, no matter how big or small. I know he made a lot of sacrifices for me, but he never complained. Or made me feel like a burden. Instead, he did everything in his power to show me that I was his number one priority." Hope swallowed past the lump in her throat. "He even called me his blessing."

Anna squeezed her hand again. "Of course you were his blessing, Hope. Just as I'm sure he was to you."

"Yes, he was," Hope murmured and manage to smile through the onslaught of tears currently blurring her vision.

"Gram," Alex called out, the interruption keeping Hope from bursting into tears as he and his brother bounded into the kitchen. "We're hungry."

"You just had breakfast an hour ago."

"I know," Zach drew out the word. "But I'm starving." He

wrapped his arms around his stomach to emphasize his ravenous state.

A twinkle gleamed in Anna's brown eyes at Zach's theatrics, but there was no mistaking how crazy in love she was with both her grandsons. Hope wondered if Anna'd feel the same way about the baby she was carrying.

Her third grandchild.

Absently, Hope rubbed her hand across her belly as Anna rose from her chair.

"All right," Anna capitulated. "How about some milk and a few cookies?"

Their little faces broke into twin beams of sunshine. "Chocolate chip?" Alex asked, his voice hopeful.

Nodding, Anna poured two glasses of milk and lined a plate with about half a dozen cookies. "That should tide you over until it's time to eat." She handed Alex the plate and carried the drinks into the great room herself.

"They're adorable," Hope said when Anna returned to the kitchen.

"They're spoiled rotten is what they are," Anna returned, adoration shining in her warm amber eyes.

"They're lucky to have you. I'm sure it's been difficult since their mother passed."

Anna glanced toward the family room where the boys were sprawled on the sofa, eating their cookies and watching Macy's Thanksgiving Day parade. "Yeah. We prayed hard for Olivia to beat it, but the cancer was too aggressive. Losing her was devastating for everyone. Especially Reese."

Hope's heart broke for them all. She knew firsthand what it felt like to lose someone you were closer to than anyone else in the world. At least Sam had lived a long and fulfilling life, whereas Olivia's had hardly begun.

"Can we have more cookies, Gram?"

"And I thought my boys had hollow legs," she said, grabbing four more cookies from the jar and handing them to Zach before returning to the table. "Speaking of my boys, I want to thank you."

Hope arched a brow. "Thank me? What on earth for?"

"For Drew being here for the holidays."

Still puzzled, Hope gave her head a little shake. "*He* asked *me* to come," she clarified.

"I know. But if you hadn't agreed, I'm pretty sure he'd still be in Kentucky right now."

Surprised by Anna's declaration, Hope was trying to formulate a response when Drew's grandparents blew into the kitchen. "Ham's here!" Zeke announced, his booming baritone reverberating off the walls and granting Hope a much appreciated but likely temporary reprieve.

CHAPTER EIGHT

By four, everyone who'd gathered at the Blackwood table for Thanksgiving dinner was stuffed to the gills. After Sarah and Zeke arrived, the three women finished what was left to get the meal on the table while Zeke took the boys out to locate the rest of the Blackwood men.

Once everyone had returned to the main house, showered, and changed clothes, they all took their seats and bowed their heads as Zeke offered the blessing from his perch at the far end of the table.

As the Amen was chorused, Eli, seated at the other end of the long oak table, carved the turkey, and from there, the food made its rounds, plates were filled to overflowing, and conversation stalled as everyone enjoyed the vast array of delicious homemade food.

Twenty minutes into the meal, small talk began to fill the silence. There was an enviable easiness among them as they chatted, teased, joked, and boasted with each other. No topic within reason was off limits, and Hope could imagine how entertaining mealtimes must have been when Drew and his brothers were growing up.

Then again, she figured anytime they were together was entertainment at its finest.

Well, maybe not so much for Reese these days. Although he had chimed in on a few of their stories, his comments had been few and noticeably brief. Hope could empathize with him. Although her first Thanksgiving without her father wasn't easy, being with the Blackwoods made the transition much easier to bear. Maybe Drew had known what he was doing when he'd invited her to come home with him instead of potentially spending the holidays alone.

Which reminded Hope of Anna's earlier comment that if Hope hadn't agreed to come to Beaumont with him, Drew wouldn't have come either. Something told Hope his mother might be right.

By the time the table had been cleared, dishes washed, and leftovers stashed in the fridge, the men retired to the great room to watch football on the big screen TV. When Hope and Anna joined them, Jack was pulling on his jacket. "You're leaving?" Anna asked, her tone laced with a hint of disappointment.

"Yeah. I promised Tess I'd stop by her parents'." He dropped a kiss on his mother's cheek. "Everything was delicious, as always," he complimented. "Hope, I'm sure I'll be seeing you again while you're here."

"I hope so."

After a round of hugs and a chorus of goodbyes, Jack left, and Sarah entered with a stack of circulars. "Are you a Black Friday shopper, Hope?"

"No. In fact, I've never done the whole Black Friday thing," she confessed. "My father and I usually got our tree and put it up instead." God, she was going to miss that.

"Anna and I venture out every year. You're more than welcome to join us if you'd like."

Though she appreciated the invitation, Hope didn't think she was ready to delve into the chaos surrounding Black Friday shopping. First, she hated large crowds. Second, she detested waiting in line. And third, Hope wanted to shop for the majority of the gifts she needed in the quaint little shops on Main Street.

"Thanks for offering to include me, but if you don't mind, I think I'll pass."

"Of course, dear. Lord knows it's not for everyone. Anna and I get a charge out of it, though, don't we?"

"Never a dull moment, I'll say that much," Anna agreed.

When Hope and Drew finally returned to the apartment, it was nearly eight. They'd eaten dessert, watched football, warmed the leftovers, cleaned up the remnants, and watched more football until halftime of the second game. At that point, the crowd gathered at the main house began to dwindle.

Reese had taken Alex and Zach for evening rounds. Holden had disappeared to a post-Thanksgiving destination he chose not to share. And Sarah and Anna had headed out for their annual Black Friday excursion, which seemed to begin earlier and earlier each year, according to Eli.

"You don't think I upset your mother and grandmother when I begged off going shopping with them, do you?"

Drew tossed his keys on the end table and shrugged out of his shearling jacket. "No, why?"

"I just don't want to offend them."

Taking her coat, he hung his and hers on the hooks by the door. "You didn't offend them."

She hoped not. The last thing Hope wanted was to appear ungrateful. Especially after the wonderful day she'd had with Drew and his family. Unsure of what to do or say next, she unnecessarily straightened the afghan on the back of one of the recliners as Drew picked up the remote. "Are you planning to finish watching the game?"

"I figured I'd turn it on. Unless there's something you'd rather watch."

Hope shook her head. "No. I was just wondering." She

turned to the fridge. "I'm gonna get some milk. You want anything?"

"Milk's good."

Great job with the scintillating conversation, Hope berated herself as she grabbed two tumblers and poured their drinks. When she joined him, Drew had removed his boots and was sprawled on one end of the sofa, his socked feet crossed at the ankle on the glass-topped coffee table. Hope handed him the milk and sat in the opposite corner, one leg curled beneath her. "Your family's a lot of fun."

"Yeah, they're quite a crew." Fondness laced his words. "But they mean well."

"I think they're great." Hope flicked a piece of lint from the khakis she'd changed into after helping Anna prep for dinner. "With Sam, people were always around, but it was different than with your family. I envy the affection and closeness you all share even when you're yanking each other's chain."

Drew smiled, and Hope's heart did a little thumpity-thump. "It's been that way my whole life."

She took a sip of her milk. "You were right, you know."

He raised a brow. "About what?"

"It did help to spend Thanksgiving here with your family instead of in Kentucky with all the memories of my dad. And missing him like crazy." Hope swallowed past the lump in her throat. "I still missed him, but it wasn't as brutal as it would have been if I were back home."

Shifting to face her, Drew smiled again, and the warmth in his beautiful eyes felt like it reached right in and touched her soul. "You and my mom seemed to hit it off pretty well."

"You were right about that too. There was no awkwardness between us at all. We worked together as if we'd been doing so our whole lives. Your grandma too." Hope took another sip of milk. "Your mother is a remarkable woman."

"Yeah, she's pretty tough to beat."

No question about that, Hope decided. To have raised four boys while also helping her husband establish a law career and run a successful horse and cattle farm, there was no doubt Anna Blackwood was one tough cookie. But Hope had seen a softer, gentler side of her today. Like when she tended to the needs of her grandsons. Or smiled proudly, if not a bit emotionally, when her eyes settled on each of her sons, all seated around the dinner table together for the first time in Hope had no idea how long.

"Can I ask you a question?"

Drew nodded. "Sure."

"Would you have come to Lone Oaks if I hadn't agreed to come with you?"

By the look on his handsome face, Hope could tell it wasn't the question he'd expected. As if he needed to formulate his response carefully, Drew didn't answer right away. After a few moments, his broad shoulders lifted and fell in a shrug. "I don't know." He met her gaze. "Why?"

Since there was no need to reveal the conversation she'd had with his mother, Hope could have chalked it up to plain old curiosity. But for some reason, she didn't. "Your mother thanked me today. When I asked her for what, she said for you coming home. I told her you'd asked me to come with you, and she said if I'd refused, she was pretty sure you'd still be in Kentucky."

Hope ran her finger around the rim of her glass and kicked herself for even starting this conversation. "It doesn't really matter," she inserted quickly. They'd entered uncharted territory here, and Hope didn't think she was ready to navigate the full depth of these waters just yet.

"It must have mattered, or you wouldn't have asked." Leaning toward her, Drew reached out and twirled a loose piece of her hair around his finger, his eyes locking with hers. "I knew the holidays would be hard for you without Sam. That's the reason I gave myself for asking you to come home with me. But when you initially refused my offer, my disappointment was more about us being apart."

Her breath caught and her heart pounded like a jackhammer against her ribs. Hope wondered if Drew could hear it. Feel it, even.

"Guess that makes me a selfish son-of-a-bitch, doesn't it?"

"Your intentions were good."

"You know what they say. The road to hell is paved with good intentions."

Smiling, Hope held his gaze. "Is that what you think you've done by bringing me to Lone Oaks? Paved a road to hell?"

Drew shook his head. "No," he answered, his voice thick. "I'm glad you said yes because I really don't know what I would have done if you hadn't agreed to come." He tucked the strand of hair he'd been toying with behind her ear, the back of his knuckles grazing her cheek. "But I do know it would have been hell leaving you in Kentucky."

Hope's stomach bottomed out. "Why?" she heard herself ask in a voice hardly more than a whisper.

"Because I would have been miserable here without you."

Every nerve in her body ran amok beneath the surface of her skin, the impulses manifesting from acute awareness to gripping fear to everything in between. Never had she felt more unsettled.

Or more alive.

Frozen in place, Hope had no idea what to do or say.

"And, just to be clear, that has nothing to do with your father or the baby," Drew added.

Immobilized by not only his words but the intensity of his beautiful blue eyes, Hope had no idea what to do or say. Hell, she could barely breathe, let alone even try to speak.

"I know we've blamed what happened between us on emotional overload and liquid courage. But regardless of how or why it happened, the truth is I wanted to be there with you that night, Hope. To comfort you, yes, but I'd be lying if I said I didn't also want to make love with you."

His words pierced her heart with the force of an arrow. Hope shouldn't have been surprised. The attraction between them had been strong from day one. Simmering on a slow boil. Teasing and taunting. For so long, they tried to ignore the pull. To keep a tight rein on their feelings. And they were successful until the one night neither of them had the strength to fight the temptation a moment longer and sought solace in each other's arms.

Maybe that wasn't all they'd found that night. Maybe they'd found something more. Something deeper. Stronger. More powerful than either of them ever expected.

Now, here they were with so much on the line. A friendship. Working relationship. One night of passion with the ache for more. And a baby they'd created in the process.

So much had changed in their lives in the last four months. Changes requiring them to make monumental decisions affecting their future, with one of the biggest being where Drew decided to hang his shingle at the end of his six-week return to Lone Oaks to fulfill his grandfather's wishes.

And if Hope decided to keep the baby, where Drew lived and worked would significantly impact her life as well, especially if he chose Virginia. Damn, she hated this. Hated how careless they'd been. Hated making decisions when everything seemed so far out of her control. Where there were no guarantees.

The more cautious and protective part of Hope's psyche urged her to pack up and get the hell out of Beaumont before things became any more complicated between them. But the part that was pure woman yearned to stay and see where the road she and Drew were on right now might lead.

It could be an interesting ride.

And might even be well worth the risks.

But should she dare take the chance?

Hope looked at Drew, her gaze locking with his. Tonight, good, bad, or indifferent, she wanted to be the woman attracted to this man. "I wouldn't want you to be miserable, so I'm glad I decided to come along with you."

"So am I." His slow grin set off a swarm of dive-bombing butterflies in her belly. "Besides keeping me from being miserable without you, you've also kept the matchmaking duo from their quest to fix me up with every available woman in the tri-state area." He cocked his head to the side. "Of course, it does put you in their direct line of fire."

His blue eyes glimmered as his grin deepened. "Are you sure you're ready for that?"

"They're your family," Hope reminded him. "So, the real question is...are you?"

Leaning closer, Drew cupped the back of her neck and pulled her toward him, his eyes never leaving hers. A warmth curled through every one of Hope's girlie parts and beyond. "Oh yeah," he murmured, low and deep. "I've been ready," he added before capturing her lips with his own.

Arrows of white-hot desire shot through Hope. Electrifying, searing, and scorching every cell until she feared she'd be consumed by the fire raging to life inside her.

Drew nipped at her lower lip, coaxing her mouth open. His tongue entered and tangled with hers. Somehow, he'd had the wherewithal to remove the glass of milk from her hands, setting it unsteadily on the end table before closing the gap between them until their lips and tongues weren't the only parts of their bodies touching.

Her soft curves molded against the rock-solid hardness of Drew's chest. Her nipples pebbled against the fabric of her bra as a desperate need throbbed relentlessly through her core.

Could he feel what his touch did to her?

———

Drew's mouth plundered hers—tasting and devouring, taking everything she was willing to give yet demanding so much more.

His hand searched for the hem of the baggy sweater Hope wore over her khakis. He wanted—no, *needed*—to feel her skin beneath his fingers. For far too many nights, Drew had lain awake, remembering how soft and pliant her skin had been the night they'd spent together. How she'd trembled. Shuddered. And quaked.

Under the sweater, Drew's fingers brushed against the waistband of her pants, stilling suddenly when he realized the button was already undone. Easing his lips from hers, his eyes opened and met Hope's. She read the unspoken question in his eyes.

"I haven't been able to fasten most of my pants for a couple weeks now," she admitted and lifted the end of her shirt to reveal the tiny baby bump. Taking his hand, she placed it on the slight roundness of her belly and laid her hand on top of his, her eyes studying him.

As much as he didn't want to break eye contact with Hope, Drew couldn't keep his gaze from drifting to where their joined hands rested atop her navel. Something shifted inside him. He felt it as keenly as he felt the warmth of her flesh beneath his palm.

The air backed up in his lungs, clogging his throat. Inside Hope was life. One they'd created together. A part of them both. Gently, he moved his hand over the slight bulge, and a tightness clutched his chest. His heart swelled as waves of love, pride, protectiveness, and gratitude coursed through every cell of his being.

Where the button was undone, his hand stilled before pulling on the tab of the zipper. His eyes lifted to Hope's. "I want to see." His voice was raw and full of emotion.

With a wobbly smile, Hope nodded. "It's easier if I stand up."

Rising, she began to lower the zipper. Drew stilled her hand. "Let me. Please."

Hope dropped her arms, and Drew pulled the zipper down, moving his hands to the sides of her hips, to push the khakis to the middle of her thighs. She wore white cotton panties, the waistband riding below the roundness of her belly. Slowly, he moved his fingers to the center of her abdomen and splayed his hands across her skin.

Drew had never experienced anything of this magnitude. Part of him was inside Hope. Developing and growing. He could see the swell of evidence. Feel it as his hands glided over her stomach in soft, slow strokes. There was so much he wanted to say, needed to convey to Hope, only he couldn't seem to push the words past the thickness clogging his throat.

The backs of his eyes burned. He could hardly breathe. Hope was having his baby. *Their baby.* The knowledge of that alone humbled him.

Sliding closer to where she stood before him, Drew caressed the small mound of flesh with his thumbs as he knelt in front of her and placed his lips against her skin. Her scent, clean and fresh with a hint of vanilla, enveloped him as he wrapped his arms around her waist and laid his head where his lips had just been.

He felt Hope's breath hitch before she wound her arms around him, holding him close. In that moment, Drew felt like the luckiest man on the planet. "Thank you."

"For what?"

"For coming to Lone Oaks." His eyes dropped to where his hand was on her belly. "For this." He eased back and looked up at her. "I don't have the words to tell you how I feel right now."

Hope smiled again. "That's good." She threaded her fingers through his hair. "Because right now, you don't need any words." Hitching up her pants with one hand, she reached for his hand with the other.

Realization slowly dawned on him. "Are you sure?"

"I've never been more sure of anything in my life."

Rising, Drew held her dark gaze. "What about the baby?"

"The baby will be fine."

"I don't want to do anything to hurt you." He laid his hand proactively on her womb. "Either of you."

"You won't." She tugged on his hand. "Now, come to bed with me."

She didn't have to ask him again.

The door to the bedroom had no more than closed before Drew had Hope against it, his mouth seeking hers. Again, he found the hem of her shirt, pushing it up until his fingers brushed the underside of her bra. He cupped the fullness of her breast.

Hope pressed herself against his palm, inviting more of his touch. Drew's breath caught in his throat. But it was her whimper against his lips that had him drowning.

His mouth left hers to blaze a trail along her jawline. Across to her ear. Down the slender column of her neck. His fingers slid inside the cottony fabric of her bra. Pushing it aside, Drew removed the barrier between Hope's flesh and his own.

For a moment, all he could do was look at her. Awed and fascinated. Her breasts were larger, rounder, and fuller than before. From his medical training, Drew knew the ripeness was pregnancy related, and he couldn't help but swell with pride knowing her transformation was a result of the seed he'd planted inside her.

Hope curled her arms around his neck, pulling his lips back to hers. She pressed her body more intimately against his. Drew groaned as his fingers caressed. His mouth devoured. And his loins throbbed.

God, how had he survived the past few months without touching her? Tasting her.

More. He had to have more. Deftly, Drew pushed Hope's

shirt over her head, tossing it aside. His lips replaced his hands, his tongue lapping and circling one nipple as he laid her gently on the bed and aligned his hard length against the softness of her luscious curves.

Suckling, he laved each breast while Hope untucked his shirt, her fingers kneading the muscles of his back, her touch a flame shooting through him like a bullet. He moved his hands across her belly. Over the edge of her khakis. Along the curve of her hip until landing at the apex of her thighs.

When she began to writhe beneath him, arching against his palm, Drew feared he might disintegrate into a ball of flames.

Lifting his head from his feast at her breast, Drew maneuvered himself so he could see her face. His heart stuttered. She was so damned beautiful. He brushed a wayward piece of hair away from her cheek, his eyes never wavering as he pressed his lips to hers.

Softly.

Reverently.

Completely.

"I've wanted to kiss you like that for months."

Hope shifted, the movement allowing him to settle more tightly against her. "Is that all you wanted to do?" she asked as her hips began a slow grind against him.

A moan he couldn't have prevented to save his life surfaced from somewhere way down low inside him. "No," he growled.

Hope's lips joined his. She invited his tongue to join hers in the dance the lower half of their bodies had already begun. "Me neither," Hope confessed, wrapping her legs around him.

"You're not playing fair, Hope."

"Are you complaining?"

"I don't want to rush things with you," Drew admitted, dropping his forehead to hers.

"I think that ship has already sailed."

Lifting his head, he looked deep into her eyes. "You know

what I mean." Sighing, he propped himself on his forearms to take some of his weight off her. "I don't want to play on your vulnerabilities either. Especially after what happened before."

Her brow crinkled. "I'm not sure I understand."

He pulled in a deep breath. "This morning, when Holden and I were mucking out the stalls, he was yanking my chain about you. When I insisted we were only friends, he said if that were the case, I wouldn't have any objections to him asking you out."

"And do you? Have objections?"

"I wanted to bash his head against the iron bars on the stall door."

Hope giggled, then covered her mouth with her hand. "I'm sorry."

Relief washed over him. "I refrained from beating him into a coma but advised him against asking you out. Of course, he wouldn't let it drop, reminding me that I'd just said we were only friends, so what would it matter. Then I reminded him about how you'd recently lost your father and didn't need the likes of him playing on your emotions."

"Aren't you the gentleman?"

"This time, I'm really trying to be," he replied. "Sometimes, I worry I took advantage of you that night. I know both our emotions were raw, but yours so much more than mine. I probably shouldn't have made love with you that night, Hope, but God help me, I'm not sorry we did."

Reaching up, Hope cupped his face in her long-fingered hands and smiled so sweetly it made the ache within him start to throb all over again. "Neither am I," she whispered as they shifted to their sides, facing each other. She laid her head on his shoulder.

There were so many things she could have said. Drew had already contemplated most of her options. But never once did he allow himself to consider she'd say she wasn't sorry either. He had assumed she had regrets. Lots of them. Especially since their one night of passion had resulted in a pregnancy she hadn't factored into her life.

At least not at this point. And, most likely, not with him.

That she wasn't sorry about their lovemaking gave Drew a glimmer of hope for their future. Still, he didn't want to rush anything. Not again. They had once, and even though they both fessed up to not having regrets, Drew didn't want to tempt fate a second time.

Besides, they weren't the only ones to consider any longer. Now, there was the baby. Another life dependent on them to make better choices.

Though Drew wanted nothing more than to finish what they'd begun, he didn't want to muddy the waters of where their relationship went from here. Assuaging the physical need winding them both tighter than a drum wasn't a risk worth taking.

Not yet, anyway.

"So, what happens now, Drew?" Her voice was soft, low. Her palm was splayed against his chest, her cheek on his shoulder.

He wished he had the answer. Right now, all he knew was that he wanted Hope with him. To get to know her as a man gets to know a woman he craves more than his next breath. To spend time with her. Talk about anything and everything with her. To prove he was worth the risk.

For the next five and half weeks, they'd have time to explore the facets of their relationship and make important decisions regarding their future.

Together.

Drew shifted so he could see Hope's face. "How about we use our time here to get to know each other better? Just do what comes naturally and see what happens."

"You just put a stop to one thing that comes quite naturally," Hope pointed out.

"Because I don't want our physical attraction and compatibility to overshadow everything else."

"Some men wouldn't care about that."

"I'm not like most men, Hope. Not when it comes to you." His gaze fell to her abdomen. "Or our little nugget." Drew raised his eyes back to hers. "So, what do you say? Are you willing to use this time in Virginia to explore our relationship beyond the pregnancy factor?"

Hope nodded. "Yeah. We can do that."

Relieved, Drew pressed a kiss to her forehead before retrieving the shirt she slept in. "Let me help you get dressed for bed."

One dark brow arched, challenging him. "That could prove dangerous."

"We'll have to force ourselves to be strong."

Pulling her off the bed, Drew slipped the nightshirt over her head, and Hope pushed her arms through the sleeves. The material slid to mid-thigh. She removed her khakis and tossed them into a corner. He took her hand and led her to the side of the bed where she'd been sleeping.

Smiling, Drew stripped to his boxer briefs and slid into the bed beside Hope, curling himself around her. With her back to his front, Drew draped his arm across her waist, splaying his hand over the swell of her abdomen. He nuzzled her neck. "Have you felt any movement yet?"

"No." She laid her hand over his. "From everything I've read, I could start to feel something anywhere between sixteen and twenty-five weeks. With the first pregnancy, it's generally not as early. Mainly because the feeling can be attributed to many things, which makes it more difficult to recognize."

"Do you want to know if it's a boy or a girl?"

"I don't know. Maybe. What about you?"

"Kind of. When can we find out?"

"Around twenty weeks, I think."

Drew snuggled Hope closer. "You'll let me be there, won't you?"

"Of course."

"Should you see a doctor while we're here?"

"Not unless there's a problem. I saw my OB before leaving Louisville and explained that I'd be out of town for a while. She said everything looked good and I should be fine until I get back. I have an appointment in early January. They'll probably do an ultrasound then."

"I'd like to be there."

When she nodded, Drew pressed a kiss against her cheek. "Good night, Hope."

"Good night." She burrowed in closer to him and interlaced her fingers with his.

After what had just transpired between them, they were off to a damn good start.

CHAPTER NINE

Hope awoke to the heavenly scent of coffee. Stretching, she raked her tangled hair away from her face and pushed herself out of bed. The need for her one cup of caffeine overrode a bathroom stop. There was no doubt she looked like a hot mess, but she was sure Drew had seen her looking far worse after they'd spent a night nursing a sick horse or assisting a mare through a difficult delivery.

Or even a night of unbridled passion fueled by way too many tequila shots.

She found Drew seated at the breakfast bar reading the morning paper and nursing his own mug of liquid energy. His hair was damp and finger-combed away from his handsome face, but the dark scruff of the beard he hadn't shaved shadowed the hard line of his jaw. He was already dressed in jeans and a flannel shirt. His feet, however, were bare.

Hope wanted to devour him.

Dang!

Then she remembered how bedraggled she must look in comparison. How was it fair that he sat there looking so sinfully sexy while she undoubtedly looked like she'd been sent for and couldn't come? Where was the justice in that?

She was about to duck back into the bedroom when Drew spotted her. "Good morning, beautiful," he greeted, his smile as bright as the sunshine streaming through the casement windows.

Damn him.

"Mornin'," Hope mumbled, heading straight for the coffeemaker. She popped in a pod, pulled a mug from the cabinet, and slid it into place before hitting the brew button, all while keeping her back to him. "How long have you been up?" she asked as the machine gurgled to a stop.

"Since about six." Rising, Drew crossed to make himself another cup of coffee. While waiting, he lifted her chin with his forefinger and dropped a kiss on her lips. "How'd you sleep?"

"Good." She sighed. Shivers rippled through her as the woodsy smell of his soap enveloped her. Never had Hope been as attuned to a man's scent as she was Drew's. Then again, every freaking thing about him affected her.

It was both unsettling and comforting at the same time.

"Want some breakfast?" he asked.

"I could eat."

"Great. I'll throw something together while you get ready."

She took a sip of coffee. "Ready for what?"

"If I tell you, it won't be a surprise."

Intriguing. Hope's pulse kicked up a notch. "A surprise? What kind of surprise?"

"A secret one." Drew opened the fridge and pulled out a carton of eggs. "Wear something comfortable and warm."

"C'mon. At least give me a hint."

"We'll be outside." He grinned, and Hope nearly swooned. "The sooner you get ready, the sooner you'll find out," he prompted when she just stood there.

What on earth was he up to? According to the conversations after dinner the day before, everyone seemed to have their own plans for today. Zeke needed to catch up on some paperwork. Anna and Sarah were off to shop Black Friday sales till they dropped. And Reese had the boys to look after while he took care of his farm chores.

Apparently, whatever Drew had planned only involved the two of them. Anticipation and excitement trembled through her.

"You're not getting ready," Drew pointed out, a glint in his lake blue eyes. "Do you need some help with that?"

"I think I can handle it." Not that she wasn't tempted.

Drew inclined his head toward the bedroom. "Then handle it," he prodded with another one of his sexy-as-hell grins.

"Oh-kay." Hope drew out the word with a mock salute and headed for the bedroom.

———

Unsure of how long what he had planned would actually take, Drew decided to prepare a big breakfast to tide them over into early afternoon if they weren't back by noon. As the bacon and sausage sizzled in separate skillets, Drew scrambled half a dozen eggs, zapped frozen pancakes in the microwave, and popped canned biscuits in the oven.

When everything was almost finished, he tried to replicate his mother's gravy by stirring flour and milk into the pan with the sausage. As the roux bubbled under medium heat, Drew dished up the eggs and set the bacon on a paper towel-covered plate. Turning back, he quickly stirred the gravy, lest it stick, before setting the table with the necessary plates and utensils.

Drew was pouring the gravy into a bowl when Hope returned to the kitchen and went to the fridge to pour herself a glass of milk. The scent of her body wash, shampoo, and something uniquely Hope reached him first, its warm, vanilla aroma curling around him like a morning glory around a beanpole.

Instead of her usual one single plait down the middle of her back, Hope had braided her hair on each side of her freshly scrubbed face, the banded ends falling just below her shoulders and brushing against a navy cable knit sweater. His gaze drifted appreciatively over the way the stretch fabric of her dark leggings molded to the curve of her hips and mile-long length of her legs before disappearing beneath well-worn black riding boots.

With massive effort, Drew restrained himself from peeling Hope right out of her clothes and hauling her back to bed. Damn, he had it bad.

"You expecting company?" Hope asked as she sat down at the table he'd laden with enough food to feed a small army.

Drew cleared his throat, hoping the evidence of his arousal wasn't as noticeable to Hope as it was painfully obvious to him. It was crazy. For five years, they'd spent an inordinate amount of time together, sometimes in very close quarters as they tended the horses in their care. But it wasn't until after they'd slept together that most of his waking hours were spent jonesing for her like some horny pimply faced teenager.

"I don't know how long we'll be out this morning, so I wanted to make sure we didn't starve before getting back for lunch."

"No worry about that." Hope shook out the napkin onto her lap. "I had no idea you were so talented in the kitchen."

Drew dropped into the seat across from her. "My talents are wide and varied and extend to many rooms in the house." He waggled his eyebrows lasciviously.

"Good to know," Hope acknowledged with a twinkle in her eye. She pulled apart a biscuit, drizzled gravy on one side, and slathered butter and grape jelly on the other. "So, what's this big adventure you planned for today?"

Drew chewed the forkful of eggs he shoveled in his mouth and washed them down with a gulp of coffee. "You aren't going to give up, are you?"

"Nope." Hope shook her head. "So you might as well just tell me." She gave him her best puppy dog look. "Please."

"Okay." He released an exaggerated sigh. "Since it is the day after Thanksgiving, I thought you'd like to go in search of a Christmas tree."

If he'd grown two heads and started spitting fire, he couldn't have stunned her more.

Yesterday when Anna and Sarah had asked if she wanted to accompany them on their shopping spree, Hope remembered admitting she'd never been to the stores on Black Friday. That she and her father usually spent the day after Thanksgiving finding and decorating the perfect tree.

Had Drew heard them?

Apparently so, dingbat.

Hope's heart swelled. "That is so incredibly thoughtful." She reached out and squeezed his hand. "But since I'm sure your mother and grandmother will have trees, it isn't necessary for us to have one here too."

Drew turned his hand over and threaded his long work-roughened fingers through hers. "You don't want a tree?"

"I didn't say that. I just don't want you to go to any extra trouble on my account."

"It's no trouble." Drew smiled, the gesture crinkling the corners of his sparkling eyes. Hope's stomach took a long, slow roll. "Besides, maybe *I* want a tree."

"Do you?" Considering he always had something else to do when they decorated the clinic, Hope doubted it.

Drew popped the last bite of his breakfast into his mouth and rose from the table. "What *I* want is to take *you* to get a tree," he murmured before leaning over, grabbing her chin in his hand, and kissing her hard on the lips. "Now, finish eating so we can get going," he instructed with a wink.

Hope polished off the remainder of food on her plate and joined him in the cleanup. "You sure are bossy lately," she accused sans malice.

"Sometimes, you need a little direction," he teased, grinning.

While Drew washed the dishes, Hope transferred the remnants into plastic containers. They'd be eating breakfast leftovers for a week. "You know what would be fun?" she asked, leaning a hip against the counter to his left.

Drew's eyes roamed over her seductively. "I can think of a lot of things that would be fun." Leaning toward her, he nipped at her bottom lip. "What'd *you* have in mind?"

"To bring Alex and Zach with us to get a tree."

The stunned look on Drew's face was absolutely priceless. "Are you serious?" The way he drew out the three words indicated he, in no way, expected her to suggest bringing his nephews along on their Christmas tree hunt. Hope also didn't think he was too keen on the idea either.

Not. At. All.

Hope smiled impishly. "Yeah."

Drew rolled his baby blues.

"C'mon, Drew. I doubt Reese has even considered getting a tree."

"My parents will have a tree. And I'm sure my mother will let them help pick it out and decorate it like she did when we were kids."

Hope laid her hands on his forearms. "Maybe, but the boys are probably bored and antsy today with your mother and grandmother out shopping. I bet Reese would appreciate a little help. Besides, kids are what make Christmas extra special."

Drew's eyes never wavered from hers. "You aren't playing fair again."

Hope nibbled the inside of her lip as she cocked her head to the side. "Is that a yes?"

The corners of his mouth tilted a fraction. "I guess," he conceded. Despite the rueful shake of his head and dramatic sigh, Hope noticed the glimmer in his eyes. "But you owe me."

Her insides tingled. "I promise you won't regret it," she replied, flashing him her brightest smile.

He kissed her. Hard and quick. "And I'll be holding you to that."

———

They found Alex and Zach in the machinery barn, "helping" Reese change the oil in one of the tractors. Since he didn't want to mention anything to his nephews about going on the Christmas tree-fetching expedition before clearing it with their father, Drew pulled Reese out of the boys' earshot to make sure it was okay first.

Reese couldn't have been more relieved. Once Drew informed Alex and Zach of his and Hope's plan for the day and invited them to come along, both boys pleaded with Reese to agree.

"You'll mind your manners and do what your Uncle Drew and Hope tell you?"

Their dark heads bobbed up and down. "We promise," Alex solemnly vowed with an elbow nudge to his little brother. "Don't we, Zach?"

"Yeah, we promise." Zach crossed his finger over his chest as if that was all it took to make their assurance legit.

"Then I guess it'll be okay."

Alex and Zach jumped up and down with unadulterated excitement punctuated by "yays" and high fives between the brothers. Just witnessing their elation made Drew glad Hope had suggested bringing the boys along.

"You sure you two realize what you're getting yourselves into?" Reese asked, his voice low amidst his sons' whooping and hollering.

No, Drew wasn't sure about much of anything. Well, other than how elevated the energy level of his surprise excursion promised to be with Alex and Zach in tow. Even then, he hadn't expected going from zero to Mach three million by simply issuing the invitation.

Still, seeing his nephews so excited made Drew glad Hope had made the suggestion.

"We'll be fine," Hope answered for them. Obviously, she was much more confident than he was. Smiling, she elbowed him in the ribs, which Drew correctly interpreted as his cue to offer his brother reassurance as well.

"Yeah," he obliged. "We'll be fine."

A flicker of amusement lit Reese's eyes for a hot second. "If you say so," he murmured before returning his attention to the tractor.

It took about twenty minutes to drive out to the section of Lone Oaks dense with coniferous and deciduous trees in every size, shape, and form. The exact spot where his parents brought him and his brothers to pick out their Christmas trees for as long as Drew could remember.

Once he stopped the truck, everyone tumbled out. The boys, still vibrating with excitement, hadn't stopped jabbering since they'd left the barn. If only they could bottle all that energy, no one in the Blackwood family would ever have to work another day in their life.

"Zippers up," Hope instructed when they were all standing by the pickup, awaiting their directions.

Both boys gave Hope the eye roll all children seemed to master at an early age but they complied without any fuss.

"Gloves?" Hope plucked a pair from her shearling jacket and slid her hands into them as Alex and Zach reluctantly did the same with theirs. "Hats?" she prompted, pulling a knit cap down over her own head. The two braids dangled past her shoulders, and the only part of her face still showing was from her eyebrows down.

"Do we haveta?" Alex bemoaned.

"Yes. You *haveta*," Drew answered as he yanked a baseball

cap on his own head and shaded his laser blue eyes with a pair of wraparound sunglasses.

"Good job, men." Smiling, Hope slid her own Ray-Bans into place. "Okay, Uncle Drew. Lead the way."

More than anything, Uncle Drew wanted to haul Hope against him and kiss her senseless. But under his nephews' hawk eyes, Drew decided that wasn't the brightest idea if he didn't want to be bombarded with a boatload of questions he was in no way prepared to answer. Instead, he hefted the chainsaw and the rest of the tree-cutting equipment out of the pickup's bed. He handled the bundle of rope to Alex. "How about you carry this?"

As if he'd just been handed over the crown jewels of the kingdom, the seven-year-old beamed and threaded his arm through the loop, adjusting the knotted portion on his shoulder. All something he'd likely seen his father or grandfather do a hundred times.

"What about me?" Zach wanted to know.

With nothing else left to carry, Drew was forced to do some fast thinking. "I'm gonna need you to have all your strength later when we have to carry the tree back to the truck. So, for now, maybe you could hold onto Hope's hand since she's never been here before."

"So she don't get lost or fall down?"

"Exactly. Think you can handle that?"

Zach's blue eyes brightened. "You bet," he assured his uncle and slipped his little gloved hand into Hope's.

"Glad you're on board to help." He smiled at Zach before turning his attention to include the rest of the trio. "We'll start up this side." He pointed to his left. "We're looking for something about as tall as Hope."

Alex and Drew started walking a few paces ahead of Zach and Hope, but it wasn't long before Zach increased his stride to keep up with his brother. Within minutes, he let go of Hope's hand and joined Alex in an all-out race to the top of the modest slope. Neither boy had bothered to scan the trees on their sprint up the hill, and in their haste, they'd passed quite a few that met the height requirement Drew had given.

"I found one," Zach announced proudly about five minutes later. "C'mon, Uncle Drew. Look."

Although a nice enough tree, it was a few inches too tall and also one of about a thousand others they'd considered as they trudged through the heavily wooded area in search of the *perfect tree*. Whenever they'd come across one that met Drew's specifications, one of his three companions invariably found something wrong with it.

Too tall. Not tall enough. Too full. Not filled out enough.

After about forty minutes of searching coupled with what felt like five miles of hiking, Drew began to think they'd never find a tree on which they would all agree when Zach announced for the nine hundredth time he'd found *the* one.

While Hope, Zach, and Alex inspected the Douglas fir, Drew hung back, waiting for one of them to find the flaw negating the tree's suitability, thus sending them off in a different direction to continue their search. At the rate they were going, they might not be back to Lone Oaks before Christmas.

Drew watched the three of them walk around the tree, eyeballing its height and width and inspecting for gaps in its foliage. When none of them said anything, Drew stepped forward. "What's wrong with this one?" he asked, knowing there had to be something.

Hope shook her head. "Nothing I can see. What about you guys?" She turned to Alex and Zach.

"Looks good to me," Alex offered his two cents.

"Me too," Zach concurred.

Hope turned to Drew, her eyes bright and her mouth—yes, the one he'd fantasized most of the morning about devouring —dimpled into a megawatt smile. "I think we've found *the* one."

Yeah, Drew was beginning to think the same thing. That he'd finally found *the* one. His heart slammed to a halt as the idea took hold. Drawing in a deep gulp of cold air, he decided he'd wait until later to wrap his head more fully around that thought. Now, they needed to concentrate on cutting down the tree and hauling it back to his grandparents' basement, where Drew had no doubt the need to decorate the fir was bound to prevail.

After all, what good was a tree if it wasn't laden with ornaments and lights?

"You're sure?" Drew asked just to make sure no one had changed their mind during his epiphany.

The three of them nodded.

"Okay. Let's cut her down."

Priming the chainsaw, Drew pulled the cord, and the small engine roared to life. After he instructed them all where to stand and what he needed them to do, Drew positioned the saw near the ground and cleanly sliced the trunk in two while Hope and Alex kept the tree from toppling by pulling on the rope Drew had attached near the top.

After he'd trimmed some bottom branches and cleaned up a few scraggly boughs, Drew, Alex, and Zach took hold and carried the tree down the hill with Hope following behind, lugging the chainsaw and rope. Once they reached the bottom, they, or mostly Drew, hoisted the tree into the bed of the farm truck. Then, everyone piled into the cab for the drive back to his grandparents' house.

"Are ya gonna put the tree up today?" Zach inquired.

"Maybe." Drew was surprised the question hadn't been asked sooner.

"Need any help?" Alex inquired, his blue eyes bright and hopeful.

When Drew looked at Hope for confirmation, she was already nodding her head with a smile. The tug on his heart intensified.

The afternoon before, when Drew overheard Hope telling his mother and grandmother about how she and her father always got their tree and decorated it the day after Thanksgiving, Drew decided to do the same with Hope today. At the time, Drew's plan did not include his nephews.

Though initially disappointed when Hope had suggested inviting Alex and Zach along, Drew now understood her reasoning. Like them, Hope also faced the holiday season without a parent for the first time. And just like Drew wanted to keep Hope's family custom alive, she wanted to help keep the boys' Christmas traditions as normal and constant as possible too.

Drew brought her hand to his lips, silently thanking her for having a heart big enough to include two little boys spending their first Christmas without their mother. "Yeah, we're probably going to need some help." Drew squeezed Hope's hand and met his nephews' eager faces in the rear-view mirror. "You wouldn't happen to know anyone who might be interested in giving us a hand, would you?"

"We would!" they volunteered quickly, loudly, and quite clearly, leaving no doubt about their willingness nor their energy level to do the job. Their reaction pleased Drew, but it was the brilliant smile Hope bestowed upon him as she threaded her fingers through his that completely melted his heart.

CHAPTER TEN

By two o'clock, they'd informed Reese of the plan to decorate the tree, choked down lunch with a speed that begged for an attack of killer indigestion, unearthed several boxes of Christmas decorations stored in Reese's attic that he insisted they use instead of buying new, and positioned the tree in the corner of his grandparents' basement apartment to the right of the entertainment center.

Once secure, all four of them stood back to look at the full-bodied Douglas fir. It was perfect.

"Can we start?" Obviously a rhetorical question, since Alex didn't wait for an answer before he was popping the lids off the plastic tubs and tossing them aside in his haste to get the show on the road.

"Here's some lights," the seven-year-old announced. "Can we put on colored ones?" he asked. "Mom said we could last year, but then she got sick, so we only had the tree at Gram's. And her lights are all white." His little brow furrowed as he looked up at Drew. "We're still gonna have a tree at Gram's, aren't we?"

Drew nodded and ruffled his nephew's hair. "You know

Gram always gets the biggest tree. I'm sure she has the one she wants already picked out."

Hope's heart broke a little more as she watched relief wash over Alex's adorable face. After having his life upended by the untimely death of his mother, it was only natural for Alex to seek consistency and normalcy wherever he could find it. Since Gram had always had a tree, it was important to him that nothing disrupted that tradition. Not even if it meant foregoing colored lights on a tree he'd had so much fun helping to pick out.

"Hey, Alex, I found our ornaments," Zach piped up, holding a box he'd dug out of one of the containers. He pitched the lid on the sofa and fished out a glittery snowflake made of Popsicle sticks. "I made this in preschool," he announced proudly before rummaging for more.

The box overflowed with every imaginable decoration an elementary school-aged child could make using construction and tissue paper, beads, pipe cleaners, clay, and wood. There were wreaths, angels, bells, reindeer, Christmas trees, Santas, snowmen, and many more holiday-themed items, each with its own story and holding its own cherished memory.

Hope's father had also kept a box of all the handmade ornaments she had made throughout her childhood. Apparently, both he and Olivia knew how meaningful those keepsakes would be for all the Christmases to come.

"Momma always let us trim the bottom of the tree with our stuff," Alex informed Hope and Drew. "And she never ever moved anything either. Even when Zach put everything in a clump. She just left it there."

Now the sadness in Hope's heart filled her eyes. All she wanted to do was haul both boys into her arms, hold them tight, and soothe away their sorrows. It wasn't fair. At least Sam had been in her life for thirty years. Alex and Zach were barely given a chance to know their mother, let alone create the years of lasting memories Hope and her father were so blessed to make.

It just about tore her already bruised heart in two.

Not wanting to put any kind of damper on their festivities, Hope knelt on the floor beside Alex and Zach as they sifted through the container. She listened to their stories about every decoration and how old they were or whose class they were in when each one was drawn, constructed, colored, or painted. Hope wondered about her own child and the stories he or she would have to share about their crafts.

As Hope listened to the joy in Alex and Zach's voices and watched the utter delight beam across their adorable little faces, she realized how much she didn't want to miss these moments with the child she carried. No, Hope wanted all of this. Wanted to be a part of those memories. To cherish every single one all the days of her life.

How had she ever considered giving her baby up for adoption? *Because you're afraid*, that little voice inside her head answered. Scared shitless was more apt, but what new parent wasn't? Besides, fear was a hell of a lot easier to overcome than regret.

Her gaze drifted to Drew. By keeping the baby, their lives would forever be intertwined. But just how would he fit into their lives? Would he go with them to find the perfect tree each Christmas? Help make ornaments? Bake cookies? Be a part of their decorating on the Friday after Thanksgiving?

And what about the other holidays? Would he help dye and hide Easter eggs? Make Valentine boxes? Go trick-or-treating? Attend every event no matter how often or varied? How involved would Drew actually be?

Especially if he chose to remain in Virginia and she returned to Kentucky. Six hundred miles was a long way to travel for every holiday, horse show, music recital, and sporting event.

Six hundred miles was a long way period.

"Are we gonna put colored lights on the tree?" Alex broke into Hope's thoughts.

Again, Hope looked at Drew, who was patiently untangling the strands of lights while she and the boys took their walk down memory lane. When their eyes met, the expression on Drew's face indicated all this was new territory for him as well.

Wrinkling her nose, Hope silently implored Drew to decide. This was his family, not hers. As a guest and someone who understood very little about children, Hope didn't want to screw anything up by making the wrong decision, even if it only amounted to what color lights to put on the tree.

Since they were both clearly out of their comfort zone, maybe it would have been better if she and Drew had done this whole tree thing without the boys.

"Well?" Alex prompted. Their gazes shifted expectantly from Hope to Drew.

"Sure," Drew finally decided and pulled the last string free of the knot. "Let's plug 'em in and make sure they're all working. Then we can get them on the tree."

That was all it took. As Hope exhaled a sigh of relief, the boys scrambled to their feet and rushed over to help Drew with the light check. Every bulb on every strand glimmered in a medley of green, blue, red, purple, and gold. Whoops of delight accompanied by fist pumps prevailed as Drew began to wrap the lights around the tree.

When it came time to decide on which decorations to use, another dilemma presented itself. Did they use the boys' ornaments or the more generic collection? Definitely generic, because the handcrafted decorations should grace the tree at the main house for all to see.

Hope looked up at Drew. "Your mother doesn't have a themed tree, does she?"

The confusion on Drew's face was priceless. "What the hell is a themed tree?"

Laughing, Hope shook her head. "Never mind. You just

answered my question." Which she should have realized, since Anna Blackwood didn't remind her of a woman who would have a flocked tree decorated with color-coordinated ornaments, garlands, and bows.

"Our trees were always full of stuff like that." Drew nodded in the direction of the bin with all the boys' homemade goodies. "Or keepsakes Mama has collected or been given over the years. Souvenirs from vacations. A big ol' hodgepodge."

"A tree full of memories," Hope preferred to call it.

Drew nodded. "Yeah. Pretty much."

"Good." She turned her attention to the boys. "Since you're staying at your Gram's, you'll probably want to put your ornaments on the tree at the main house so you can see and enjoy them while sharing them with everyone who visits during the holidays, right?"

Zach looked at Alex for confirmation. "Yeah. Gram's tree is always ginormous. There'll be lots of room."

And if there wasn't, Hope had no doubt Anna would find the space. "Okay, then, let's search for what we can use on this tree," Hope suggested as she and the boys sorted through several of the other containers.

The door at the top of the steps opened. "Everyone decent?" Zeke bellowed, his booming voice startling Hope and prompting both boys to race toward the staircase.

"Pops! Come look at the tree. Uncle Drew and Hope took us to get it, and we're helping them decorate it and ev'rything," Zach announced.

"And they said we could put colored lights on it too," Alex added.

"I can see that," Zeke replied as he allowed his great-grandsons to drag him toward the tree for a closer look.

"What'dya think?" Alex wanted to know.

"I think it's the best-looking tree I've seen this year," he complimented with exactly the right amount of enthusiasm and admiration. "You're gonna put some decorations on it, aren't ya?"

"A'course, Pops." Zach rolled his blue eyes at what he considered an absurd question. "You wanna help?"

"Wish I could," he answered, and Hope thought he really did look sorry that he wouldn't be able to lend a hand. "But I gotta go tend to a sick horse at O'Malley's." He shifted his attention to Drew. "I know I said we'd start Monday, but I was hoping you'd be able to come along on this one."

"What seems to be the problem, Pops?" Alex asked.

"She's trying to foal, only it's not time yet." His gaze returned to Drew. "I'm likely to need some help."

Drew nodded. "Sure." He stopped short, as if realizing that would mean cutting out on the tree-trimming festivities with Hope and the boys.

"Good. I need to check some things in the truck. Come on out when you're ready." With that, he headed back up the stairs.

"Boys, why don't you go ahead and start hanging some ornaments where you can reach while I help your Uncle Drew gather what he needs to help Pops."

Happy to oblige, Alex and Zach jumped right to the task.

Drew followed Hope to the door. "I'm sorry about this," he apologized, grabbing his coat and hat off the hook. "And I have no idea how long this might take," he added as he pulled on his jacket.

"Don't worry about that," Hope assured him. "Will it be okay for the boys to stay here while you're gone? Or should I take them back to Reese?"

His brows knitted together. "Are you okay with them staying here?"

"Sure. It's just that it's been less than a week since Reese even met me. I'm not sure I'd be comfortable leaving my children in the care of a virtual stranger."

"They've been with us all day."

"Right. *With us.* Your brother entrusted them into *your* care. Not mine."

Laughter made the dimples in Drew's cheeks deepen, the corners of his eyes crinkling. "It's more likely he only entrusted them to me because he knew you were going to be with us, considering my level of knowledge on the care of anything outside of the four-legged variety is pretty slim."

But you've been taking excellent care of me for weeks. It was true. Even before her father's diagnosis, Drew always seemed to look out for her in some capacity. Lately, though, he'd really gone above and beyond.

"I don't want him to think..."

"He's not going to think anything," Drew assured her. "Besides, we'll likely be back by dinner. He isn't going to come looking for them before then."

"Are you sure?"

Drew lifted Hope's chin with his finger and dropped a kiss on her lips. "I'm positive." He rubbed her nose with his. "I'm sorry to leave all this on you."

Hope smoothed the front of his jacket with her palms. "Don't worry about that either. We'll have lots of fun, I'm sure."

Leaning forward, Drew kissed her again, a little longer this time. Hope's toes curled inside her boots.

"If it looks like it might take a while, I'll call you."

"Okay."

"Hope! Come see what we've done so far," Alex called from the other room.

Drew pulled the hat on his head. "She's coming," he yelled back. With a wink, he headed out to join his grandfather.

When Hope returned to the living room, Alex and Zach had placed about half the red, gold, blue, and silver ornaments on the branches they could reach, which was about the lower one-third of the tree. So far, they'd done an excellent job spacing out the bulbs to use as much of the tree as possible.

But even if they'd clumped everything together in the back of the tree, Hope never would have said a word.

Or moved a thing.

That the boys were enjoying themselves was all that mattered. If they wanted to hang the ornaments upside down while standing on their heads, Hope wasn't about to stop them. Just like she wouldn't dare stop her own child when the time came for him or her to help with decorating their home for the holidays.

The mere thought gave Hope the warm fuzzies.

For the remainder of the afternoon, Alex, Zach, and Hope finished decorating the tree. In addition to the colored balls, they added glass bulbs in many shapes and colors and a variety of other unique ornaments and decorations."

When there wasn't another spot to even hang a piece of tinsel on the heavy-laden Douglas fir, Hope stood back to admire their work. It was absolutely one of the most beautiful trees she'd ever seen, and she knew it was because of the enjoyment Alex and Zach had gotten from helping.

"Well, what do you think?" Hope asked.

"It's awesome!" Alex exclaimed as he edged closer to Hope's left side.

"I love it!" Zach curled against her right side, holding an angel. "Do you think we should wait and let Uncle Drew put the angel on top?"

Hope smiled at Zach's thoughtfulness. "I think he'd like that."

Alex nodded. "Yeah, me too. Dad always used to put the angel on top of our tree when we lived at home."

His words sliced straight through Hope's heart. What could she possibly say to that without dissolving into a puddle of tears? Since she had no idea how she'd explain why she was bawling her eyes out to the boys, Hope inhaled a deep breath and exhaled slowly. Then, she changed the subject entirely.

"Okay, men. Let's vacuum up these needles and add some water to the tree."

"I'll get the vacuum," Alex volunteered as he ran to the closet by the outside door.

"I'll get the water," Zach followed suit.

Upon their return, Hope showed Zach how to crawl behind the tree and add water to the metal stand. With that task completed, Alex started vacuuming.

"How's that?" Alex asked over the roar.

"Perfect."

"We gotta put this around the bottom," Zach held up a red tree skirt edged in white.

"We sure do."

"I can do it." Alex tried to grab the furry material from his little brother.

Zach held on tight. "So can I."

Fighting between siblings. More uncharted territory. As an only child, Hope had no experience whatsoever on this front. But with both boys digging in their heels and pulling the tree skirt in a tug of war, Hope needed to intervene sooner rather than later.

"How about we do it together?" She stepped in between the feuding brothers to take the skirt from both their grips.

"How we gonna do that?" Alex furrowed his little brow, reminding her of Drew. Hope wondered if their child would inherit the same mannerism. She hoped so.

"Well?" Alex prompted.

"You take this side." Hope handed Alex one end and turned toward Zach. "And you take the other. Now get down on your knees and crawl under the tree, bringing the ends with you. I'll be in front making sure it stays straight."

They did as she instructed. "Okay," Alex informed her from his spot under the tree. "Do we hook it together in the back?"

"Yes, attach it where the Velcro is."

"Got it," Zach shouted.

Hope smoothed out a few wrinkles in front. "Okay, try to back out without knocking anything off the tree."

Gingerly, or as gingerly as two energetic boys can manage, Alex and Zach commando-crawled backward, careful not to rise too high until their heads had cleared the bottom branches. Both sat on their haunches. "Now what are we gonna do?" Zach wanted to know.

Hope looked around the room at the explosion of plastic containers, lids, empty ornament boxes, and shredded paper. "I think we definitely have some cleaning up to do," she answered, bracing herself for their fervent protests.

Only none came. Instead, both boys nodded, not overly enthusiastically, of course, but in agreement nonetheless. Hope decided to run with it before they changed their minds.

In less than an hour, everything was packed back in the containers, which they carried to the garage, leaving the one with all their ornaments by the door, so they wouldn't forget to take it with them. Returning to the living room, Hope vacuumed up the remaining debris, and the boys returned the step stool to the closet.

"Now what?" Zach reiterated his favorite question after the vacuum had been put away.

"Now, we fix some dinner and then sit down to admire our work." While Alex and Zach might be blessed with an unlimited energy supply to keep going and going, Hope was positively pooped.

"We'll help!" Zach squealed, running to the kitchen. "What're we havin'?"

"How about grilled cheese?"

"That's my favorite," Alex declared.

"I like macaroni and cheese the best."

Hope rummaged through the cupboards and fridge to locate the bread, cheese, butter, and some boxed mac and cheese. "It's not going to be homemade, so this will have to do."

"It's my second-best favorite," Zach stated.

Both lent Hope a hand, helping to assemble the sandwiches, measuring the water for the macaroni, and setting the table. Forty-five minutes later, everything had been cooked, devoured, and cleaned up. With juice boxes in hand for the boys and a glass of milk for Hope, they headed to the living room and curled up on the sofa to watch a Disney movie Alex had found on TV.

Ah, finally, Hope thought, a little rest for the weary.

CHAPTER ELEVEN

It took nearly three hours, but between Drew, Zeke, and Daniel O'Malley, they were able to deliver the mare of her foal. Unfortunately, there was nothing they could do to save the prematurely born colt, but at least there hadn't been complications that would put the mare at any further risk.

They stayed to inject the horse with a healthy dose of antibiotics, made sure she expelled all the afterbirth, and gave O'Malley explicit instructions for her care and what to watch for during the next forty-eight hours. Both Drew and Zeke told the horseman not to hesitate to call if anything didn't look right.

Once back in Zeke's dual-wheeled pickup, Drew caught the water bottle his grandfather tossed him and downed half of it in one swallow. "Guess that wasn't the best first impression I could have made, huh?"

Zeke drove away from the main stable. "Why? Because the foal didn't make it?" He cast a sidelong glance at Drew. "You know as well as I do if we couldn't stop the labor, there was no chance of saving the foal. It was too early. O'Malley knows that."

"I know, but it still sucks when it happens."

"You can't save 'em all, Andrew. I hope you've learned at least that much in the eight years you've been working in Kentucky at that fancy horse clinic of yours."

Drew's lips twitched. It didn't matter that Wakefield was one of the most renowned and well-reputed equine clinics in the country. In Pops' eyes, the facility was just another animal hospital located in a different state from where his grandson belonged. "Yeah. I've managed to figure a few things out."

"The important thing is we saved the mare. And that was all you. " Zeke pointed a finger as thick as a cigar at Drew. "She was getting weaker by the second, and she'd never have been able to deliver on her own. You pulled that foal, saving her a helluva lot of extra work and her life in the process. That's a damned sight more important to O'Malley than saving the foal."

Drew realized his grandfather was right. But no matter the circumstances, the odds, or the bright side, Drew hated to lose an animal. "Yeah, he told me she comes from a good line. I'm hoping there aren't any complications precluding her from foaling in the future."

"You think there might be?"

Shaking his head, Drew finished off the water. "I didn't feel any internal tears or abnormalities. If she gets back on her feed in the next few hours and no infection sets in, she'll probably be fine. She's healthy and strong. For some reason, her body just rejected this foal."

"Best she lost it, then," Zeke concluded as he turned toward Lone Oaks. "Nature's way of taking care of things."

Drew thought about Hope and their baby, fear instantly gripping him in a stranglehold. What if there were complications with the pregnancy or problems with the baby and nature simply took care of things? Hell, they didn't even know if it was a boy or girl yet.

No! Drew refused to consider any alternative other than a healthy pregnancy and birth for both Hope and the baby. So far, everything seemed to be progressing right on schedule. And Drew would do everything in his power to ensure that continued.

No matter what.

"Your girl sure is a beauty," Pops' voice broke into his thoughts.

"Hope?"

"You bring another girl home with you we don't know about?"

Drew laughed. "No. She's the only one." He'd wondered when Zeke would get around to inquiring about Hope and their status as a couple. He was surprised it had taken this long. "But she's not really my girl." At least, Hope didn't consider herself as such. Which made Drew wonder how she viewed her role in his life.

Co-worker?

Friend?

Baby mama?

Regardless of what labels he or Hope might assign to their relationship, being the mother of his child was indisputable

Zeke shot Drew another sidelong glance. "How many other girls you ever brought home with you?"

"There were plenty of girls around when we were growing up, Pops."

"Plenty of girls who found *their* way to Lone Oaks," Zeke corrected. "I don't remember you actually bringing any of them."

As usual, his grandfather was spot on in his observation. Growing up, neither he nor any of his brothers needed to bring any girls to Lone Oaks. Most had no trouble making their own way to the farm on the pretense of coming to see the horses and cattle.

Except for Tess, Jack's best friend. She was always there. Like a part of the family.

"How long have the two of you known each other?"

"About five years."

"Five years?" Zeke shook his head. "Damn, boy, what the hell are you waiting on?"

Drew tried not to laugh. "Not everyone moves at the same pace as you, Pops." If Drew had heard the story once, he'd heard it a million times—how as soon as he'd laid eyes on the lovely Sarah Jane Holden, there wasn't anyone or anything going to stand in Zeke's way of making her his bride.

And he hadn't. Within a month, the two exchanged vows, and next February, they would celebrate their fifty-eighth year together.

"No point wastin' precious time when what you want is standing right in front of you. Might be something you want to think about." He shook his white head again. "Five damn years," he scoffed. "What if she'd met someone else?"

A definite concern, for sure. One Drew wrestled with more than a few times over the years. "Hope has a rule about dating the men she works with," he answered. "She doesn't."

"Rules are made to be broken, boy."

Yes, they certainly were. The baby Hope carried was proof positive of exactly how well aware Drew was on the matter. "She *did* agree to come here with me."

"That she did," Pops agreed as he drove under the iron Lone Oaks arch.

"But it's all still new territory. So behave yourself, old man."

Zeke laughed, a deep and rumbling sound from low in his gut. "I don't think it's me you're gonna need to worry about. I imagine your Mama and Grandmama are already abuzz with plans."

Yeah, Drew had no doubt about that.

When Pops pulled up in front of the ranch house, Reese was getting out of his pickup. "Y'all been on a call?" he asked as the three of them met in between the trucks.

Zeke nodded. "Yeah. Preterm foal at O'Malley's." He

clapped Drew on the back. "My old bones are tired. See you boys tomorrow."

As their grandfather ambled toward the back door, Drew turned to Reese. "I left Hope with the boys. They were helping her decorate the tree."

"They probably worried the hair off her, Drew. You shoulda brought 'em back to the main house."

"Funny. She was worried you wouldn't feel comfortable having them stay with her since you only met her a few days ago."

Reese toed the gravel beneath his boot and shook his dark head. "I figure she must be okay if you brought her here all the way from Kentucky."

Their gazes locked. "She is."

"I know you said you asked her to come with you because her daddy recently passed and it would be her first holidays without him, but I have a feeling there's a little more to it than that."

With anyone else, Drew would adamantly deny anything more than a friendship existed between him and Hope. But this was Reese. His big brother and Irish twin. Growing up, they'd been each other's sounding board and confidant. Sure, the years Drew was away at college and working at Wakefield put somewhat of a strain on their bond, but nothing could sever it completely.

Just like there was no way Drew could lie to Reese about his feelings for Hope. So he didn't even try.

"Yeah. There is." Drew wanted to tell Reese about the baby, but he'd promised Hope they'd wait till the time was right. With their relationship still tenuous at best, Drew didn't want to run the risk of upsetting her.

"Are you in love with her?"

That was a damn good question. "She matters to me, Reese. More than any other woman ever has." Drew plowed his fingers through his hair. "Is that love? I don't know. All I do know is that I can't imagine my life without her in it."

Reese clapped a hand on Drew's shoulder, and the raw pain shadowing his brother's eyes floored him. But it was Reese's words that totally gutted him. "Then don't waste precious time, Drew. If there's one thing I've learned in the last year, it's that."

When they stepped inside the basement, Alex rounded the sofa in his stocking feet and put a finger to his lips. "Shhh!" he whispered, then pointed to the couch where Hope was curled on her side, her right hand tucked beneath her cheek, and her left resting on what Drew knew was the gentle swell of her belly.

The sight alone took his breath away.

And in that moment, he knew. He was in love with Hope Logan. Completely and irrevocably. Now and forever.

He wondered if she might ever feel the same way.

To keep her from waking up to find all of them staring at her, Drew beckoned Reese and the boys into the kitchen. "How long has she been asleep?"

"Well, the movie's almost over, and she didn't even make it through the first song. Why? Didja want us to keep her awake?"

Drew chuckled. "No. I appreciate you guys letting her sleep. She's been kinda tired lately." And after traipsing through the snow to pick out a tree and then spending the rest of the afternoon decorating it with his nephews, she had to be exhausted.

"Boys, get your coats and boots. We need to get back to the main house before Gram sends out a search party for us."

"Want us to wake Hope up so we can thank her and tell her goodbye?" Zach's blue eyes were hopeful.

Reese shook his head. "No. You can thank her tomorrow when you see her."

Nodding, both boys hid their disappointment as they sat

on the floor to pull on their boots. Jumping up, they grabbed their coats, zipping themselves into them with quick precision. "You gonna let her sleep on the couch all night, Uncle Drew?"

"Probably not," he answered and didn't miss the faint grin barely touching his brother's lips.

"Well, when she wakes up, tell her thanks for the grilled cheese and mac and cheese."

"And for letting us help decorate the tree," Alex added.

"Will do," Drew promised.

"C'mon, boys," Reese prompted, holding open the door.

"Wait. We have to take this box of ornaments to Gram's." Hefting it, Alex carried it past his father with Zach scrambling after him.

Tugging his hat farther down on his head, Reese shot Drew a rusty grin. "When she wakes up, be sure to thank Hope for me, too, Uncle Drew."

CHAPTER TWELVE

Drew debated whether to risk waking Hope by moving her to the more comfortable bed or leave her to continue sleeping on the sofa. Since he needed to wash the muck off from O'Malley's, Drew opted for the latter. If she was still asleep when he finished, he'd decide what to do then.

The hot stinging jets of the shower gloriously pelted the aching muscles in his shoulders and back. Pulling a foal was never an easy task, but it became brutal when trying to pull one from a weakened mare who'd already expended most of her energy trying to deliver on her own.

Drew wished they'd been successful in stopping her labor and giving the foal a few more weeks to develop in utero. But like his grandfather said, they'd saved the mare. He just hoped she came through the next forty-eight hours without any complications.

Shutting off the taps, Drew stepped out of the shower and quickly toweled himself dry. Under different circumstances, like if he were alone or going straight to bed, a pair of boxer briefs would suffice. No problem. But he wasn't alone, and as inviting as the bed looked, his growling belly overruled his need for sleep.

Drew pulled on a pair of flannel sleep pants and a clean tee-shirt before emerging from the bedroom. Hope was still asleep, curled in the same position with her hand resting on her belly. His heart filled, swelling inside his chest. Drew resisted the urge to gather Hope in his arms. Just to hold her. Protect her. Confess how much she meant to him.

And always would.

But after the full day she'd had trudging through uneven terrain searching for the perfect tree and then wrangling two rambunctious little boys, she needed her rest more.

So, Drew headed to the kitchen and rummaged through the fridge, deciding the quickest and quietest supper he could prepare was between two slices of bread. Grabbing the supplies, he slapped together three thick sandwiches of bologna, ham, and salami topped with tomato, lettuce, and mayo.

Once he poured himself a glass of milk, Drew carried his plate to the small table and sat down to devour his makeshift dinner. He'd just polished off the last bite of his third sandwich and was carrying his dishes to the sink when Hope shrieked.

"Boys!" Scrambling to her feet, her eyes wide with panic, she frantically looked around the room searching for his nephews. Her hair was smushed down on one side of her head and a sleep mark creased her right cheek. Drew had never seen anything more beautiful in his life.

"Reese took them home about an hour ago," Drew enlightened her.

Releasing a huge sigh, Hope patted her palm against her breastbone as if the gesture might calm down what Drew suspected was a galloping heart. "I'm so sorry. We sat down to watch a movie after we finished eating, and I must have conked right out." She rolled her eyes. "Reese was probably horrified."

Drew wiped his hands on the dishrag and draped it over the neck of the faucet. "The boys were fine," he assured her.

"In fact, they made sure we didn't make any noise to wake you when we came in."

"At least I managed to feed them before passing out."

"Yeah, we heard all about the mac and cheese and grilled cheese sandwiches."

"Their favorites," Hope explained.

"The favorites of almost every kid in the world, I imagine."

"Were they yours?"

He gave a half shrug. "I was more partial to the mac and cheese. Especially Grandma's. But don't dare tell my mother I said that."

Hope drew a cross over her heart with her forefinger. "Your secret's safe with me," she promised. "How'd the call go?"

Pushing himself away from the sink, Drew crossed the room until he was within touching distance. He tucked his hands in the pockets of his sleep pants to keep from reaching out because if he touched her, he wouldn't want to stop. Since the day had obviously exhausted her, Drew didn't want to add to her fatigue.

"The foal was too early."

"I'm sorry."

Her wince didn't escape him. Four months ago, they were in a similar situation with a foaling mare and a colt that didn't survive. The same day her father had received his terminal diagnosis. The night they'd found comfort in each other's arms and conceived the child Hope now carried.

The child she wasn't sure she wanted to keep.

"Is the mare all right?" Hope's question broke into his thoughts.

Drew nodded. "If no infection sets in, she should be fine."

"Good."

There were smudges under her eyes. Not too dark, but noticeable enough to concern him. "You still look tired." Drew reached out and smoothed an errant strand of hair behind her ear. He couldn't help himself. The pull toward her was that strong. "We should have split getting the tree and decorating it into two separate days. Doing both today, especially with Alex and Zach, was too much."

"I'm fine. My OB and everything I've researched on the internet indicates it's perfectly normal to be more tired when pregnant. The baby takes everything it needs first, so I get whatever's left over." Hope smiled. "Other than a waning energy level, I feel perfectly fine."

Taking her hand, Drew stretched out on the sofa and tugged her down beside him. "I still should have taken the boys back before heading out with Pops. Then you could have rested sooner."

"It didn't really hit me till we sat down to watch the movie. Besides, I had fun with Alex and Zach today." She smiled again, and Drew could have sworn his heart skipped a beat. "I think they had a good time too."

"I'm sure they did." And if Pops hadn't needed his help, Drew would have gladly enjoyed it right along with them. In fact, as he shifted his eyes toward the ornament-laden tree, its colored lights twinkling brightly in the dimly lit room, Drew envied missing out. "It looks great," he murmured and pressed a kiss against her temple.

As if his lips scorched her skin, Hope gasped and jumped to her feet. "Oh, I almost forgot!"

Panic shot through him. "What?"

Hope crossed the room and bent to pick up something from the other side of the tree. "Just the most important part." She extended what looked like an angel toward him.

Wow. He certainly wasn't expecting that. Drew swallowed past the sudden lump in his throat. "Dad always puts the angel on top of the tree at the main house." At least he had when he and his brothers were growing up. He assumed the tradition remained.

"The boys said Reese did the same for their tree. So, it

seems only fitting that as the dad in residence of this basement apartment, you should have the same honors."

The impact of Hope's words slammed his heart against the walls of his chest. Was she saying what he thought she was saying? Or was it just wishful thinking on his part? Drew wanted to ask but in the event he'd completely misunderstood her meaning, he feared hearing her response.

Still, his need to know overruled caution. Drew rose from the sofa. "Does that mean..." He couldn't settle on the best words for the situation.

Nodding, Hope set the angel on the table and met his expectant gaze. "I don't want to give the baby up for adoption. I don't think I ever really did." She shook her head. "I was just scared, I guess. Still am, but..."

This time instead of interrupting her verbally, Drew cupped her upper arms and captured her mouth with his. In no way did Drew want to silence Hope, because he wanted to hear everything she had to say. But right now, he couldn't formulate adequate words to convey how happy he felt, so he sure as hell hoped in this case his actions spoke louder than words.

Hope's sigh of capitulation and the manner in which she returned his kiss told him he'd chosen correctly. Drew rested his forehead against hers when their lips finally parted, and he released the breath he'd been holding for the last four months.

"You should hate me."

Drew leaned back to look at her. "Why would I ever hate you, Hope?" He narrowed his gaze with uncertainty. "Because you wanted to do what was best for the baby by considering all the options available?"

"Was I?" she challenged him as well as herself. "Or was I only thinking about myself? What was best for me and my career?"

He tucked a loose strand of hair behind her ear. "You said it yourself, sweetheart. You were scared."

Her chin quivered as she stared into his chest. "I still am."

"And rightfully so."

"Are you?" Her voice was barely more than a whisper.

"Afraid?"

Hope nodded.

"Of course I am," Drew admitted. "But I doubt we're afraid of all the same things. Or, at least, I imagine the level of our fear varies significantly."

Her eyes narrowed. "How so?"

"The difference in our family dynamics and the impact that has on our lives, for one." Drew shook his head. "Not that one is any better than the other, but how we're raised affects us. Our outlook. Our perceptions. The paths we choose. The decisions we make. Pretty much everything."

Taking her hand, Drew led Hope back to the sofa. "Tell me what scares you the most."

"In general, or with the pregnancy?"

"The pregnancy."

"Motherhood." She exhaled slowly. "Being responsible for another human being. Will I know what to do? What if I don't? What if it's too much? What if I can't handle it?" By the time she paused to take a breath, her voice trembled and tears filled her eyes, deepening the amber color.

Drew wrapped his arm around Hope's shoulder and tucked her against his side. "Don't you think most people are scared shitless when they find out they're going to be parents, Hope? Especially for the first time?"

"Does the thought of becoming a father scare you?"

"Hell, yes. Just not to the point that I'm on the verge of a panic attack about it."

"But I am."

Nodding, Drew pressed a kiss to the top of her head. "Your level of fear does appear to be much higher than mine."

Hope raked her teeth across her bottom lip. "And I assume you attribute this to the difference in our family dynamics. That, since I come from a broken home because my mother walked away without looking back when I was five, and you come from a close-knit extended family, that makes me more afraid of becoming a good parent than you. Not to mention that you still have that extended family to support you, and I'm now essentially an orphan."

"You don't think it makes a difference?"

She averted her gaze. "Of course it does."

"Different doesn't mean one is superior to the other." Drew curled his forefinger beneath her chin, forcing her to look at him. "These last few months have been pure hell for you, Hope. Having never lost a parent, I can't begin to imagine what that even feels like. But I can try to understand how everything you've been through makes facing this pregnancy so much different for you than it is for me."

Drew laid his hand on the gentle swell of Hope's belly. "What I want you to know more than anything else right now is that you're not alone. We're in this together, Hope. No matter what."

Hope covered his hand with hers. "You do realize what a hot mess I am, right?"

Relief loosened the tight bands of tension holding his body hostage. "Well, you're in luck then, because hot messes are my specialty."

A smile tugged at her lips. "Good to know."

With gentle strokes, Drew caressed Hope's belly. "This time next year, he or she will be here." He was still in absolute awe that a part of him grew inside Hope's womb.

"Do you have a preference whether it's a girl or boy?" she asked.

"Not really. How about you?" Although he'd already envisioned teaching a son to mount a horse, catch and throw a ball, bait a hook, and ride a two-wheeler, Drew would be just as enamored with a daughter, who, if she was anything like her mother, would also enjoy riding horses, going fishing, and playing ball.

"I just want him or her to be healthy."

"And happy."

"Of course." She traced several circles on the back of his hand. "Do you want to find out whether it's a boy or girl?"

Drew placed a kiss on her temple. "I want whatever you want," he replied and meant every word.

Bracing her left hand on the arm of the sofa behind him, Hope shifted to face Drew. "Are you sure about that?" A sexy gleam sparkled in her big brown eyes, and heat curled through him, settling in his groin.

In that instant, something significant shifted between them. Something neither could name but felt all the same. "Positive."

Hope inched closer, and Drew's blood throbbed like fire through his veins. "Do you know what I want right now?"

"Ice cream and pickles?"

Slowly, she shook her head back and forth. Then moved even closer, like a cat on the prowl.

"To put the angel on top of the tree?" Drew somehow managed to ask.

This time when Hope shook her head, she sank her teeth into her bottom lip and lowered her eyes to his mouth. When she smiled, his entire body shot to attention. "I give up." Drew shifted his hips to relieve the tightening in his boxer briefs. "What do you want?" His voice was raw, hardly more than a rasp as desire raged through his system like wildfire.

"You." She nipped at his lips. "More specifically, I want you to make love to me." Hope swung her legs to the floor, pushed herself off the sofa, and held out her hand.

Yes, something had definitely shifted.

His whole damn world.

Taking her hand, Drew stood and cupped her face between his hands. "No." He kissed the left corner of her mouth. "Not to you." He kissed the other side. "Only with you," he clarified before scooping her into his arms and carrying her toward the bedroom.

Heat sizzled between them, and his body pulsed with every beat of his galloping heart. Never had he felt more alive. More aroused. More everything.

He kicked the door shut, and Hope slid down the length of his body until her feet touched the floor. Unable to resist a moment longer, Drew kissed her, his tongue immediately seeking hers. Hope's arms encircled his neck, and her fingers dove through his hair. Drew's pulse roared in his ears as their tongues met and mated, each darting in, out, and around the other's. The ritual was old. Basic and primal. A prelude of what their bodies would soon replicate.

Drew dug his fingers into her hips. He pulled her close, leaving no doubt to how much he wanted her. Jolts of electricity sizzled beneath his skin wherever Hope's hands, fingers, or lips grazed. Up and down the length of his back. Over his shoulders. Down his arms.

When their mouths parted, Hope whimpered in protest. "Baby, I want you so much it hurts," Drew growled, his voice raw and ragged.

Hope slid her hands down his chest, slipping them beneath the hem of his shirt and shoving it upward. "Take it off," she demanded, her tongue blazing a trail from one taught nipple to the other.

Happy to oblige, Drew yanked his tee over his head and tossed it aside, not caring where it landed. Before he could pull her back into his arms and kiss her senseless, Hope mirrored his actions by removing her own sweater.

"My God, you're beautiful." Drew deftly flicked open the front clasp of her bra, and her full, ripe breasts spilled into his eager hands. Reverently, he caressed the lush globes, pinching one nipple between his thumb and forefinger as he captured the other with his lips and tongue.

She tasted like heaven.

"Please," Hope begged and pulled his hips firmly into the cradle of her thighs.

It took every ounce of control Drew could muster not to lose it all right then and there.

Though Drew feared he might disintegrate if he broke contact with Hope, it was a risk he needed to take to rid them of the barrier of fabric prohibiting them from becoming one. In a flurry of mutual desire and lust, they tore off the rest of their clothes until they stood together naked and wanting.

Drew's body ached with a hunger so fierce and hot he feared he might burst into flames. But he didn't want to rush anything. He wanted to savor every moment. To drink in her profound beauty. Her flushed skin and luminous dark eyes. Her swollen pink lips. Her luscious breasts, now so full and ripe from not only her arousal but in preparation to nourish the child nestled inside her womb.

Their child.

Drew had never wanted a woman more. He doubted he ever would. For him, Hope was the one.

The only one.

Now and forever.

"Make love with me, Drew. Please. I need to feel you inside me."

Brushing his knuckles lightly along the curve of her cheek, Drew curled his fingers beneath Hope's chin, tipped her face up toward his, and pressed his lips softly against hers. "I don't want to hurt you." He covered the swell of her belly with his other hand. "Or the baby."

"You won't," she assured him. "We're fine."

Drew needed no further encouragement. He scooped Hope into his arms and gently laid her in the middle of the bed he'd turned down after showering. He stretched out alongside her. First, he only wanted to look at her. Second, he wanted to touch her. And then, he wanted to taste her.

All of her. Every blessed inch.

His gaze followed the trail of his fingers. Through her dark hair. Along the graceful line of her neck. Across the tautness of her nipples. Over the dips and curves of her waist and hips. Down and then back up the endless length of her legs until finally ending at the apex of paradise.

"Please," Hope pleaded, her body writhing under his touch —urging and pleading for release.

Drew smiled. "Soon, baby," he promised, his heart full. Of Hope. Of how much he loved her. And only her. Forever.

He captured her mouth and rolled her onto her back, settling himself into the cradle of her thighs, his arousal hot against her skin. "Do you feel what you do to me?"

"Yes," she panted and jackknifed her legs on either side of his hips. "Drew, I can't..."

Gently, Drew eased himself inside her velvety folds. Hope arched to meet him. Slowly, he entered and withdrew, filling her more and more with each thrust until they established a slow and steady rhythm. His lips found hers, and their tongues danced in unison with their bodies. Their blood heated to a fevered pitch. Their needs surged, climbing toward the ultimate peak until their hearts collided.

God, he'd never experienced anything like this before. They were like two pieces to a puzzle, their fit absolute perfection.

As their pleasure intensified, Drew watched Hope's eyes melt into liquid pools of chocolate. Faster and harder now, he drove her to the edge of glory and brought her back again and again. Hope wrapped her mile-long legs around his waist and drew him inside as deeply as possible.

"More," she cried, raking her fingers down his back as she arched to meet him thrust for thrust.

And then it happened. Her body shuddered as her muscles clenched around him. Drew cried out her name a second before coming apart inside her. Their souls united into one as their worlds collided into the most glorious explosion of all time.

If they hadn't just been to paradise, they'd come pretty freaking close.

———

When Hope awakened a few hours later, Drew was spooning her, his arm draped possessively across her waist. Every inch of her body still tingled from the thoroughly spectacular love-making they'd shared before they both collapsed from sheer exhaustion.

There wasn't an inch of Hope's flesh Drew hadn't touched or tasted, bringing to life things within her that Hope hadn't even known existed, let alone experienced with anyone else. Never had she felt more alive. More wanted. More treasured.

Being with Drew was quite simply amazing.

Though she hated to move and break contact with Drew, nature was calling rather insistently. Gingerly, Hope eased herself from Drew's embrace and pushed herself off the bed. She scooped up her underwear and Drew's tee-shirt on her way to the bathroom.

Once she'd taken care of her business, Hope dressed and met her reflection in the mirror. Her hair was a tangled mess, and her dusky skin was still slightly flushed. Her eyes, dark and luminous in the light, sparkled beneath the thickness of her lashes. Her mouth, still rosy and swollen from Drew's delicious kisses, dimpled into a satisfied grin.

Unlike after their first and only other night they'd spent together, Hope wasn't on the verge of a full-out panic attack. Nor did she have the overwhelming urge to run. No, this time, there was no remorse. No what-the-hell-was-I-thinking recriminations. No desire to flee.

No, this time, Hope had no regrets. A few weeks ago, being with Drew again would have put the fear of God in her. But this time, even without the guarantee of where their relationship went from here, she had no misgivings.

For now, *this* was enough.

Flipping off the light, Hope quietly slipped back into bed. She hadn't any more than slid beneath the covers when Drew's arm snaked out to pull her against him. With his free hand, he brushed her hair to the side and nuzzled the back of her neck. "I missed you." His warm breath tickled the back of Hope's neck.

Her entire body hummed in response. "I had to pee." Hope laid a hand over his. "I didn't mean to wake you."

"You didn't." Drew kissed the spot below her ear. "Seems I have trouble sleeping when you're not beside me." He continued to kiss his way down her neck. "In fact, I've slept better the past few nights than I have in years."

Ironically, so had she, which somewhat surprised Hope, since she had never wanted anything more than the covers touching her when she slept. Yet, after sharing a bed with Drew the past few nights, where it was impossible not to inadvertently touch each other, Hope had slept more soundly than when she'd been at home in her queen-sized bed alone.

Hope couldn't help but wonder if she'd ever sleep as well without Drew beside her. After the incredible intimacy between them a few hours ago, Hope sincerely doubted it. What they'd shared had been staggering.

Magical.

Earth-shattering.

So much more than she'd ever expected. But was magnificent, toe-curling sex enough on which to build a relationship?

It's one helluva start, the little voice in her head insisted.

Okay, that much was true. Besides, they had much more in their favor than phenomenal sex and an unborn child. They had an extraordinary working relationship and shared many things in common, including their love of horses, sports, and homemade Italian cuisine. They were also friends.

"Hope?"

"Hmmm?"

"Please tell me you're not having any regrets."

Rolling onto her back, Hope met his beautiful Blackwood blue eyes. "No." She shook her head. "No regrets," she assured him.

She saw the tension in his whisker-stubbled jaw release as he brushed her hair back from her face and cupped her cheek in his hand. "There is so much I want to say to you right now."

Hope turned her lips into his palm. "Tell me without words," Hope whispered and pulled his mouth to hers.

CHAPTER THIRTEEN

By her own choice over the next few weeks, Hope kept herself quite busy at Lone Oaks. When she wasn't assisting Zeke and Drew on calls, she treated patients at Doc's clinic for small animal care, updating his antiquated record-keeping system to a more efficient, user-friendly electronic platform, and pitching in to help Anna with Alex and Zach.

As if she needed more to do, within the last week, Hope had taken on the bottle-feeding responsibility for a calf whose mother wasn't producing enough milk. And for the previous three mornings, she'd baked cookies with Sarah for the Christmas bazaar at St. Luke's. All that, combined with spending her nights having the best sex of her life and being four and a half months pregnant sometimes left Hope too exhausted to pull herself out of bed in the morning.

Today had been one of those mornings. So, when Doc called at the ass-crack of dawn to inform them of a bovine emergency at the Howard farm, Hope had begged off. Instead, she'd curled herself around Drew's pillow and drifted back to sleep.

For over four hours.

Hope couldn't remember ever sleeping this late. If so, she

must have been ill because, as the daughter of a horse trainer, early mornings at the barn or track were the norm. Even when she'd gone to college, if she didn't have an eight o'clock class, Hope was generally up by sunrise, either studying or working at one of the campus farms.

Old habits were hard to break.

Until this morning, apparently.

Stretching, Hope threw back the covers and crawled out of bed. Once she'd peed, she pulled on leggings and a thigh-length sweater, brushed her teeth, and headed to the kitchen for her one allotted jolt of caffeine. As she waited for her mug to fill, Hope sent Drew a text.

> *Sorry I bailed on you this morning. Hope everything is*
> *okay.*

Drew didn't respond until she'd sat down at the table with a slice of buttered toast and a full mug of coffee.

> *Milk fever. Early stages. Dosed her up on an IV of calcium.*
> *Will swing by later to check on her. In between regular*
> *calls now.*

With large animals, much of a veterinarian's job was with preventive care and maintenance, so visits were routinely scheduled at least twice a month and often weekly for the bigger operations.

> *Need my help?*

> *No. We only have two more.*

> *Okay.*

She felt a little guilty, but not enough to insist. Sometimes, it was nice not to be on call and allow the morning to unfold naturally.

How about we go out tonight? Just the two of us.

Little tingles of delight shot through Hope's belly.

Sounds great.

His response was a smiley face emoji with heart eyes that set off its own wave of tingles throughout Hope's entire body.

Except for the few times they'd ventured into Beaumont to have dinner with Jack and Tess, mostly their meals were eaten with Drew's parents or grandparents. Though she was grateful for the times they stayed put in the basement apartment and cooked for themselves, Hope also enjoyed spending time with Drew's family. Getting to know them. Watching the ease with which they interacted. Envying the powerful bond they shared.

And falling a little more in love with him every day.

How could she not? In the years they'd known each other, Drew hadn't ever been anything but kind to her. Even when she'd refused to go out with him, he'd respected her decision to keep their professional and personal lives separate. Despite their mutual attraction, they managed to build a strong working relationship together.

Drew also hadn't allowed anything to become awkward between them after they'd slept together four months ago. Hope didn't know what she would have done without his unwavering support during her father's illness and death. He'd been her rock. Never more than a phone call or text away. His strength sustaining her through the darkest moments of her life.

Even after she told him she was pregnant and was considering adoption, Drew hadn't made any irrational demands.

Instead, his only request had been that they discuss all their options and decide what to do together.

Though Drew never pressured her, he wasn't averse to subtle nudges. Like inviting her to come home with him for the holidays by pointing out she shouldn't be alone for her first Thanksgiving and Christmas without her father. He'd been right, of course. If she'd stayed in Kentucky, Hope would have been miserable. Hell, she probably wouldn't have bothered with a turkey or a tree.

Drew made sure she had both.

And so much more.

No wonder it had only taken a few days of being in Virginia with Drew and his family for Hope to realize she never really wanted to give up their baby. She may not have any immediate family left, but Drew did.

The more time they spent with Drew's family, the more Hope realized he was where he belonged. Here at Lone Oaks, surrounded by the people who loved him wholeheartedly and whose influence had shaped him into the man he had become. Where he could work alongside his grandfather and take over the practice when the elder vet was ready to retire. Where he would be close enough to lend his father and brother a hand or give them a break from the grueling twenty-four seven, three hundred and sixty-five days a year commitment the farm demanded.

Here, Drew would be close enough to support Reese as his brother worked through his devastating grief and help him return to the land of the living again.

Yes, Lone Oaks was exactly where Drew belonged.

And if it is, where does that leave me?

Good question. One she and Drew had successfully avoided discussing since the Friday after Thanksgiving.

Despite working, eating, and sleeping together, they hadn't talked about their feelings. No declarations of love. No mention of their future. As if by some unspoken agreement, neither dared to say anything that might break the spell they'd cast around themselves.

Yet, with over half their time in Virginia already behind them, the luxury of remaining silent waned. Sooner rather than later, decisions needed to be made, starting with where Drew wanted to continue his veterinary practice. And because of the baby, that choice alone would invariably set into motion a domino effect of decisions affecting the rest of their lives.

That was what being a parent was all about, though, right? Making sacrifices. Putting the needs of the family first. Making decisions based on what was best for the child rather than their own wants, needs, and comfort zones.

For them, it all boiled down to Kentucky or Virginia and the six hundred miles separating Louisville and Beaumont. Though Drew clearly belonged at Lone Oaks, Hope knew being a full-time father to their child would supersede all else. So, wherever their child resided, so would Drew. And that meant one of several things could happen.

One, Drew would ask Hope to relocate to Virginia with him. Although she very much liked Beaumont, and Drew's family couldn't be any more welcoming, Kentucky was her home. And despite everything she'd endured this past year, Hope wasn't sure she could leave it all behind.

Two, if she refused Drew's request to stay, he would return to Louisville with her and accept Neil Wakefield's partnership offer. Though he would be near their child, and his successful career was bound to continue no matter where he practiced, Lone Oaks was his home. And not being where he truly belonged would inevitably lead him to resent her.

Three, Drew could remain in Beaumont and petition the court for joint custody.

No. Hope shot that choice down without any further consideration. At. All.

With only three weeks till the new year, Hope realized the

time had finally come for her and Drew to break their silence and make some decisions, no matter how difficult.

A tap on the door jolted Hope from her thoughts. Setting down her coffee, she opened the door to Drew's mother. "Mrs. Blackwood. Good morning."

"It's Anna," she reminded Hope with a smile. "And good morning to you too." Her smile widened. "I hope I'm not interrupting anything."

Considering the path her thoughts had taken, Hope was grateful for the reprieve. "Not at all." She opened the door wider and stepped aside. "Please. Come in."

Once Anna was inside, she pulled off her brown leather gloves and unzipped her dark fleece jacket. "It's pretty chilly out there this morning," she declared, unwinding the bright red knit scarf from around her neck and draping it along with her coat over the back of a kitchen chair.

"Can I get you some coffee?"

"Yes. Please."

As Hope waited for the drip to finish, Anna took a seat at the table. "How do you take it?"

"Black is fine."

With mugs in both hands, Hope carried them to the table and joined Anna. "I guess the boys are still in school."

Nodding, Anna blew on her coffee before taking the first sip. "Yes. Praise the Lord." She set her cup down. "I love those boys with all my heart, but I also love to see the school bus pull up every morning."

"When do they break for the holidays?"

"Friday is their last day until after New Year's. I may need professional help by the time they go back."

Hope laughed. "They are full of endless energy, for sure."

"I've appreciated every second you've helped out with them these past few weeks."

"I've enjoyed it." And she had. Plus, it had given her a

glimpse into what to expect in a few years. "Can I make you some breakfast?"

"Heavens, no." Curling her hands around the mug, Anna leaned forward. "I suppose you're wondering why I'm here."

The thought had crossed her mind, but Hope figured Anna was either being hospitable or needed a diversion from her usual routine. "I hope it wasn't to see Drew."

"No." She took another sip of coffee. "I actually came to see you."

Yeah, that clarification did absolutely nothing to ease Hope's mind. Since there were so many directions this conversation could go, it was all Hope could do to keep her nerves from jumping straight into overdrive.

"I've alarmed you," Anna observed quickly. "That wasn't my intent."

Great, either she reads minds or my emotions are written all over my face. Hope didn't know what was worse. "Not so much alarmed as curious."

Anna's dark gaze met and held Hope's. "I don't want to come across as some meddlesome and prying old mother hen."

"But you're concerned about your son."

"A mother's curse. No matter how old they are or how far away they go, it's impossible not to worry. Eli and I did our best to give them the tools they'd need to make good decisions and become productive citizens in the world. For the most part, I think we succeeded."

"I would have to agree."

"But that doesn't explain why I'm here, though, does it?"

"I imagine you have some questions regarding the nature of my relationship with your son." What mother wouldn't?

"Just one."

Surprised, Hope swallowed hard. "Okay." Nodding, she folded her hands on the table and sat up a little straighter. "What would you like to know?" Hope asked and braced herself for Anna's response.

Her brown eyes settled on Hope. "When my grandbaby is due?"

Stunned, Hope's breath caught in her throat. Of all the questions Anna could have asked, Hope never saw that one coming. Nope. Didn't even make Hope's top one million things Anna Blackwood might want to know.

What was worse? Anna expected Hope to give her an answer, which should be relatively easy considering there was only one—May 4. Yet when Hope finally pulled herself together enough to respond, she asked a question of her own. "How did you know?"

A smile crinkled the corners of Anna's eyes. "Honestly? I wasn't a hundred percent sure until now." Her smile curved into a grin, and Hope saw Drew in the gesture. "But I was pretty confident. Obviously, huh? Or I wouldn't have just blurted out what I wanted to know."

"Probably not."

Anna set her coffee aside and reached across the table for one of Hope's hands. "I'm not here to judge, Hope."

That, at least, was a huge relief.

Still.

"What made you suspect I might be pregnant?"

"Well, having four children of my own, I recognized some of the signs."

"Really?" Hope frowned. She'd been uber careful to conceal any outward signs of her condition. At least she thought so.

Anna nodded. "As cliché as it sounds, you *are* glowing. Plus, I've never seen you drink anything but water, milk, or juice." She inclined her head toward Hope's coffee. "Your one allotted serving of caffeine, I presume?" At Hope's nod, Anna's gaze dropped to her mug. "My fourth this morning."

"I miss having more than one cup." Hope sighed before draining what was left of the single serving she did allow herself. Lately, good to the last drop held new meaning for her. "And that's all it took to pique your curiosity?"

Anna shook her head. "No. There are other subtle nuances and gestures both you and Drew have that I doubt either of you are even aware of."

"Like what?"

"Like pressing your hand to your lower back when you've been standing for a while. The silly grin on Drew's face whenever he looks at you and his eyes automatically drop to your belly. How you tug on your shirttail when you get up or sit down. The way Drew watches your every move. That sloppy grin again."

"You noticed all that?"

"And more," Anna confessed. "You're a little fuller than you were when you first arrived, especially right in front. Things no one besides a woman who's watched her own body go through the transformation of pregnancy would likely notice."

"I'm so sorry." A wave of guilt washed over Hope. This was not the way Anna should have learned she was going to be a grandmother for the third time. Once again, all because of Hope's selfishness.

"What on earth for?"

"For not telling you about the baby." Hope blew out a breath and shook her head. "It isn't because we didn't want to, but more because nothing about this pregnancy has been planned." Hope raised her hands in the air, letting them fall back to her sides. "Besides being on the same veterinary team at Wakefield, nothing between Drew and me has been planned or occurred under traditional circumstances." Tears pooled in Hope's eyes. "Until we came here, we hadn't even been on a real date."

"Life has a way of just happening sometimes."

"I considered giving the baby up for adoption." The confession tumbled out before Hope could yank the words back. Great. Just great.

Too agitated to sit, Hope pushed herself to her feet and

paced a small triangle between the living room and kitchen. "You must think I'm a horrible person. Not to mention what the hell kind of whack job your son has managed to get himself hooked up with."

"I told you I wasn't here to judge. And I don't think you're a horrible person either."

"Just a complete whacko," Hope muttered.

"Not at all." Anna bridged the gap between them. "After all you've been through the past few months, I think you're handling things pretty damn well."

Hope couldn't help but laugh. How in the world could Anna say such things with a straight face? "If you truly believe that, then maybe I should be concerned about your state of mind. Because trust me when I tell you, I feel like a ticking time bomb inside." Her voice cracked on the last word.

"And rightly so," Anna replied. "Hope, having a baby is daunting under the best of circumstances. But when combined with working a full-time job, caring for a terminally ill parent, and then grieving his loss, I can't begin to imagine the emotional roller coaster you've been riding."

No argument there. Especially considering how often Hope felt like she was going off the proverbial rails lately. "When I first found out about the baby, I was in total shock. I mean, I was already well into the first trimester and had no idea I was even pregnant. With everything else going on, it just never occurred to me."

"Which is perfectly understandable."

"I still felt like an idiot for not having any suspicions, though. Looking back, I know there are things I should have noticed. But I guess my mind wasn't on that particular frequency at the time."

"I doubt it was."

"Once the initial shock wore off, a million questions ran through my mind. But one kept surfacing." She met Anna's steady gaze. "What if I couldn't handle being a parent? My mother couldn't. What if I turned out like her? That's why I considered adoption. It was a knee-jerk reaction because I didn't want my child to have a mother like mine."

"And that by itself tells me you're nothing at all like your mother, Hope."

"But she didn't leave until I was five."

"Did you ever ask your father what happened?"

"He didn't like talking about her. But one day, when I was about twelve, I kept asking questions. Finally, he told me she wasn't cut out to be a mother. But it didn't matter because we were fine without her and he loved me enough to be both my mother and father." Emotion burned her throat and welled up in her eyes. "And he did." Sniffing, Hope swiped at her eyes. "I never asked him about her again."

"But you still worry you'll end up being like her?"

Hope nodded. "Every damn day."

"What about your father?"

Hope narrowed her gaze. "What about him?"

"Don't you think you have just as much of a chance, if not more, of being the kind of parent he was to you rather than your mother, who chose to walk away?"

Once again, Anna's response surprised Hope. Knocking her a little off guard. But making a lot of sense. "Yeah. It does."

"But you're still scared."

Hope nodded. "I know it's normal, especially for first-time parents. That *is* something Drew and I have talked about." She managed a small smile. "He's scared too."

"Of course he is. And you're right. It is normal to be tied up in knots at the prospect of becoming a parent." Anna smiled, the gesture warming her brown eyes. "When I first found out I was pregnant with Reese, I was a basket case. So was Eli. But with Drew, the fear wasn't as intense because we had some idea of what to expect."

That made sense. Everyone experienced some level of trepidation about the unknown. Having a baby wouldn't be any different. Probably worse.

The two of them returned to the table. Hope grabbed two bottles of water from the fridge, handing one to Anna before sitting down. "I want you to know I never meant for this to happen."

"You didn't get yourself pregnant, Hope. Therefore, the responsibility isn't yours to bear alone either."

"But I *am* responsible. If I hadn't found out my father was dying on the same day Drew and I failed to save a foal, we wouldn't be having this conversation. But as soon as I realized we couldn't do anything more for the colt, my world simply imploded. I couldn't breathe. Or think. Inside I felt like everything was shattering into a million pieces. The pain was excruciating. I just wanted it all to go away, to escape the reality of my situation for a little while. I should never have invited Drew to stay for pizza and Patron. Instead, I should have insisted he go home so I could drown my sorrows alone."

Hope dared a glance at Anna. "But I didn't. And that makes me responsible, because if I had made better decisions, Drew and I would have never ended up sleeping together."

A few silent beats passed between them. "Do you want to know what I think?" Anna asked but didn't wait for Hope to reply. "I think you both had choices. Drew's a big boy. And he could have left any time he wanted. That he chose to stay tells me he was right where he wanted to be."

Hadn't Drew admitted as much to Hope on several occasions? "But our choices that night continue to complicate everything else."

"Life is full of complications, Hope. Some are natural and inevitable. Some can be avoided or at least alleviated. Some, no matter what, just are. The hardest part for us is figuring out how to navigate through them while staying true to ourselves in the process."

The very dilemma with which Hope was struggling when

Anna showed up at the door. Too bad no epiphany had struck in the last forty minutes.

Well, except one.

"So much hinges on whether Drew decides to return to the equine clinic or stay here to work with Doc." Hope concentrated her gaze on tearing off the water bottle's label. "But Lone Oaks is where Drew belongs."

"Maybe."

Hope jerked her eyes to Anna's.

"A month ago, I would've agreed. Now, I'm not so sure."

"I don't understand." And she didn't.

"Oh, don't get me wrong," Anna answered. "Nothing would make me happier than to have all my boys back home. But where Drew decides to hang his shingle is not my decision. Nor is it only about what he and Zeke once dreamed about having together. Now, it's about what's best for you, Drew, and the baby."

"And since Drew's made it clear he intends to be a full-time, hands-on father, the decision falls to me by default. Because regardless of all else, Drew's choice will be to live and work wherever his child resides."

"Have you and Drew discussed this at all?"

Hope shook her head. "Only superficially. Nothing in depth."

"Then, don't you think it's about time you did?"

Hadn't Hope drawn the same conclusion earlier? "Yeah. We should. It's just..." Hope wrestled with how to articulate her biggest concern to the mother of her baby daddy.

"What?" Anna prompted.

No need to hold back now, that little voice insisted. *Not after everything else you've admitted to her today.* Hope drew in a deep breath and let it out slowly. "The complications I alluded to before? Well, a discussion on where to live and work would be a whole lot easier if Drew and I could better define our relationship."

"Ah, I see." Uncapping the water, Anna took a healthy swig before continuing. "By that, I'm assuming you mean beyond having a baby together."

Hope nodded. "Don't get me wrong. We do care about each other. A lot. But..." Hope looked down at the pieces she'd torn from the label on her water bottle, "aside from a physical relationship, we've only agreed to see where things might go while we're here for the holidays. No pressure. No expectations."

"And?"

"That's kind of where we've left things." While also continuing to have incredible, toe-curling sex, that is. But his mother didn't need specifics.

"Why?"

"Because it's easier than talking about our feelings?" Thus, running the risk of discovering the only things they had in common were a veterinary career, the baby, and the aforementioned amazing sex.

Anna folded her forearms across the table and leaned forward. "Are you worried you and Drew might not want the same things?"

Who the hell knew? Shrugging, Hope blew out a slow, shaky breath. "I don't want a relationship based on his feeling obligated or because it's the right thing to do. But mainly, I don't want either of us to make any decisions we'll end up regretting." Hope shook her head. "I just don't think that's possible."

"No, I'm afraid it's probably not," Anna confirmed with a smile. "Life would be so much simpler if we all had a crystal ball, wouldn't it?"

"Amen to that."

"We can only be expected to do the best we can with what we have, Hope. There will always be risks, some bigger and more challenging than others. More often than not, we'll be forced out of our comfort zones and be compelled to compromise more than usual. Sometimes, we just need to trust our gut, get out of our own way, pray for guidance, and have faith everything will work out."

Anna tapped her palm against the tabletop. "But I still believe if you and Drew sit down together and have a heart-to-heart talk, you'll find the decisions you need to make aren't as difficult as you're afraid they're going to be."

"I wish I had your confidence. Especially since I don't know even where to begin this conversation with Drew."

Rising, Anna slipped into her jacket, but before sliding her hands into her leather gloves, she laid her hand over Hope's and squeezed. "Just say what's in your heart, Hope. That's usually the best place to start."

Had her father been there, he'd likely have given her similar advice. Maybe he'd sent Anna in his place. Stranger things were known to happen, and with Sam Logan, nothing was beyond the realm of possibility.

As they walked toward the door, Hope wished for something to offer Anna in appreciation for initiating the long-overdue conversation about the baby, for her advice and suggestions, and especially for her kindness, understanding, and support. As Anna reached for the door handle, Hope remembered she'd never answered Anna's initial question about when her grandchild was due.

And that was when Hope realized what she could offer her baby's grandmother. "So, I was wondering if you have any plans for the first week of May," Hope asked.

Slowly, Anna turned toward Hope. "Not that I know of right now. Why?"

"Well, if you're not busy, I'd really like you to be there for the birth of your third grandchild."

Tears filled Anna's beautiful brown eyes. "Are you sure?"

"Positive."

"Then, wild horses won't be able to keep me away," Anna promised with a smile that rivaled the sun.

CHAPTER FOURTEEN

As Drew finished up the last call with Pops, his phone dinged with the personal notification tone he'd assigned to Hope.

You coming back here for lunch?

Why? You miss me? 'Cuz I can be there in five minutes.

Actually, Tess invited me to go Christmas shopping with her.

Unsure whether Hope wanted to go or was looking for an excuse to beg off, Drew tapped his reply:

You going?

I hate to say no. But not sure when we'll be back.

And in their earlier texts this morning, they'd planned a night out, Drew read between the lines.

No worries. Go have a good time with Tess.

You're sure?

Positive.

Hopefully, I'll be back in time for us to do something.

Drew grinned.

I'll be looking forward to it.

He added a googly-eyed emoji.

Me too.

Glad she felt the same way, Drew inserted a smiley face with heart eyes, but not wanting to read too much into her response, he deleted it. Still, he needed to close with something. He typed several things, erased them, and then just went with:

Be safe and have fun

He added red and green hearts.

God, he felt like a freaking teenager again.

Shaking his head in derision, Drew tossed his phone on the console and peeled off the coveralls he wore to protect his clothes. Since Hope was off with Tess for what could be a few hours or an all-day excursion, he slid behind the wheel and headed in the direction of the main house.

He was getting out of the truck when his father intercepted him. "What's up?" Eli asked.

"Hope is shopping with Tess, so I thought maybe I could persuade my lovely mother to invite me to lunch."

"I have a better idea. Why not let your old man take you into town for a bite to eat?" Eli countered.

"Shouldn't I offer to take you to lunch?"

"Whatever works." Eli rounded the hood of Drew's truck. "You drive."

"Aren't you gonna tell Mama you're leaving?"

"It was her idea. In fact, I was just about to text you when you pulled up to the house."

Not sure what was going on with his father, Drew simply nodded. "Oh-kay."

"What'd'ya say we go to The Finish Line?" Eli suggested, referring to Beaumont's hometown version of a sports bar and grill.

"Sounds good to me."

Once inside, the hostess guided them to a booth to the left of the horseshoe-shaped bar. At least a dozen TVs were anchored to the walls, each playing a different athletic event or sports commentary channel. For a Monday, Drew was surprised to find almost every table and booth, as well as most seats at the bar, fully occupied.

After a quick perusal of the menu, they gave their order to the perky brunette who introduced herself as Adrienne. Both Drew and his father opted for quarter-pound cheeseburgers, fries, and an appetizer of fried pickles. Since he might be summoned for more calls later, Drew settled for an iced tea. His dad ordered a beer.

"Looks like they're doing a roaring business," Drew commented as the waitress set their drinks in front of them.

"Yeah, it's like this almost any time Earl and I come for lunch," Eli concurred, speaking of his law partner and brother-in-law, Earl Palmer. "Or when your Mama will let me bring her so she doesn't have to cook."

"Still hard to get her to go out, huh?"

"She can be stubborn as a mule sometimes." Eli tipped the bottle to his lips and drank. "But I will say she's more agreeable to the idea lately. Usually after a full day with the boys."

"They do vibrate with an overabundance of energy, that's for sure."

Eli nodded. "Hope is great with them."

Yeah, she was. A natural, really. She was going to make a great mother. "I think they bonded when we went to get the Christmas tree, especially when they got to help her decorate it."

Their waitress arrived and set the appetizer along with two square white plates on the table between them. "Can I get you anything else right now?"

"No. We're good," Drew answered.

"Great."

"So." Eli dredged a crusted pickle through the remoulade sauce. "Are you any closer to a decision on whether you're going to stay here and work with Pops or return to Kentucky?"

Drew had wondered how long it would take before someone broached the subject with him. So far, Pops had been surprisingly quiet on the subject, as had his mother and grandmother. Hell, since the day they drove to Lone Oaks, even Hope hadn't asked him which way he might be leaning.

Not that he blamed her. Surely, Hope realized his decision would also impact her life, considering he'd made no secret of his intention to be a full-time father. Which ultimately meant his choice depended on where Hope and their child resided.

"That's quite a heavy sigh," Eli noted.

Drew had been so deep in thought he hadn't realized he'd made any sound at all. "Six months ago, the decision would have been much easier to make."

"Because of Hope?"

"Yeah." He took a sip of tea. "She's pregnant." Although they'd agreed to share the news with his parents together, Drew was very much in need of some fatherly advice right about now.

"Ah, that is a game changer." There was no censure in Eli's voice.

"Don't get me wrong. I'm not upset about the baby. To be honest, I can't believe how deep my feelings are for something I haven't seen or touched. But just seeing the swell of Hope's belly and knowing that a part of me is growing inside her..." Drew trailed off, shaking his head. "I can't begin to describe how that makes me feel."

His father smiled. "I have a pretty good idea."

Drew laughed. "Yeah. I guess you do."

"And if you think your heart is so full it could burst out of your chest right now, wait until you hear the heartbeat for the first time or feel the baby move when you put your hand over her belly bump. But nothing is more incredible than seeing your child enter the world and hearing their first cry."

Listening to his father recollect the miracle of birth hollowed Drew out. He didn't want to miss any part of that. Not one single second of the pregnancy or labor and delivery. Drew wanted to witness firsthand the developmental milestones their child mastered and to be present for all the firsts. To champion each challenge and celebrate every achievement, no matter how big or small.

More than anything, Drew wanted to share all facets of parenthood with Hope. From poop explosions to potty training, the terrible twos to adolescent angst, the first day of kindergarten to high school graduation. And every blessed aspect in between.

"I want to be a part of all that and more," he confessed.

"But," his father prompted.

"I was offered a partnership at Wakefield a couple of days before Pops called. At the time, considering Hope and the baby, it seemed like a no-brainer to accept. But Neil insisted there was no rush. That he wanted me to take some time to think the offer through before deciding anything. Then, Hope learned about the bleak financial situation her father left behind, which, as luck would have it, happened to be on the same day Pops called to pitch his idea of me coming home for the holidays."

"Damn, that's quite a trifecta. Two partnership offers and a baby to boot. Some would consider you an incredibly fortunate man."

Yeah, some would. But right now, Drew wasn't feeling so fortunate. "Working at Wakefield has given me opportunities I wouldn't have gotten here. Consequently, I've grown exponentially as a veterinarian. Before Pops called, I was convinced I wanted to focus my career solely on horses. But being here these past few weeks has made me realize I also enjoy caring for both large and small animals and working in the field as well as the clinic. I like the diversity here and the familiarity of the clients, their herds, and their family pets. Plus, who better to learn from than the master veterinarian himself?"

"There is that."

"None of that takes Hope and what she wants into consideration, though." Drew traced a line of condensation on his glass. "How fair is it to ask her to leave the only home she's ever known to come and live with me in mine?"

"Not all parents live together, Drew."

"But I don't want to be a part-time father, Dad. Only spending time with my son or daughter when I can work it into my schedule to make the six-hundred-mile trek." He raked a hand through his hair, barely resisting the urge to pull it out. "Plus, there's how I feel about Hope and the fact that I can't imagine my life without her in it."

"Have you talked about any of this with Hope? Told her how you feel?"

"Somewhat. Nothing in depth. When we first got here, we decided not to rush anything and just see where things go. Other than that, our conversations center mostly around the baby."

Drew drained the rest of his tea, wishing it were something much more potent. As if that would somehow provide the clarity needed to figure this situation out when, ironically, it was too many tequila shots that got him into this predicament in the first place.

Okay, granted, alcohol wasn't to blame for everything on his plate right now. Yes, the Patron lowered his and Hope's inhibitions, which led to them sleeping together without even thinking about using protection. But it had nothing to do with the two partnership offers on the table or the woman who owned his heart long before the night they shared over four months ago. Because even if Hope weren't pregnant with his child, Drew still wouldn't want to be separated from her.

Ever.

"Sounds to me like it's time for you and Hope to delve past the surface and have the rest of the conversation," his father surmised.

"You're right." Yet despite how much their relationship had grown in the past few weeks, Drew wasn't sure Hope's feelings for him matched how he felt about her. Or if they even came close.

Drew didn't doubt Hope cared about him. Or that she considered him more than a coworker slash friend slash baby daddy. She seemed content with how things were now, but he had no idea what that meant for their future. Although she'd agreed they would raise their child together, what exactly did that look like to her? That they'd live in the same house? Have separate residences in the same area, and if so, where would that be—Kentucky or Virginia?

"The sooner the two of you talk this out, the sooner you'll have the answers you both need to move forward."

Though his father was right again, their future, from this point forward, hinged on Hope's answer to one question— would she leave Kentucky and stay here with him at Lone Oaks?

"You okay?" Eli asked as he dumped ketchup on his fries.

Drew had been so lost in his thoughts he hadn't noticed the server arrive with their food. "Yeah. Just thinking."

"You come to any decisions?" his father asked before taking a healthy bite of his burger.

"Just one, really. But it'll be the determining factor for everything else." Drew met his father's curious stare. "I'll talk to Hope and ask her if she'll consider moving to Virginia. If she says no, then I'll be heading back to Kentucky."

Eli nodded. "Sounds fair enough."

"I know Mama's gonna be disappointed we haven't told her about the baby. More so if we return to Kentucky."

"Yeah, well, you don't have to concern yourself with telling her because she already knows."

"About the baby?" Shocked, Drew narrowed his gaze. "How?"

"She's suspected since Thanksgiving. But this morning, she decided she couldn't wait for the two of you to get around to telling her, so she went to see Hope."

For a few seconds that felt like years, Drew was rendered speechless. What had his mother said to Hope? How had Hope responded? Moreover, why hadn't Hope told him about his mother's visit before going shopping with Tess?

Fear burned through his gut as a million *what-if* scenarios lit up his brain. Like what if his mother's inquisition had upset Hope to the point she decided to use going shopping with Tess as an excuse to pack up and get the hell out of Dodge before he or anyone else in his family could stop her?

"Did Mama happen to mention how Hope reacted? If she was okay when she left?"

Eli dredged a fry through the ketchup on his plate. "The way your mother explained the conversation to me is that she came right out and asked Hope when her grandchild was due. Hope was surprised, of course, but they went on to have a lengthy chat, probably much like the one you and I are having." He popped the fry into his mouth, chewed, and swal-

lowed. "She didn't mention anything about Hope being upset."
He cocked his head to the side. "Now, your Mama is a different
story."

"What do you mean?"

"Although she's over the moon about being a grandmother
again, she is a little put out about having to find out on her
own. So prepare yourself to get an earful when you see her."

"I'm assuming our having lunch out together is you
running interference on my behalf?"

"Your mother needed a little time to settle down."

"She's that angry?"

"Not so much angry as concerned."

That made two of them. "Did Hope give her any indication
she might consider staying at Lone Oaks?"

Pushing his plate away, Eli rested his forearms on the table
and leaned toward Drew. "I'll tell you like your mother told
Hope. You'll both feel a lot better once you sit down and talk
all this out together." He signaled for their waitress. "Box that
up for him, will ya?" While Adrienne put Drew's uneaten
burger and fries into the Styrofoam container, Eli left enough
cash to cover the bill and a generous tip.

"I was gonna buy you lunch," Drew reminded his father.

Eli grinned. "Consider it my first Father's Day gift."

Father's Day. Drew shook his head, literally and figura-
tively, as the reality of becoming a father sank in a little deeper.
Anxiety snaked through him, intensifying his initial worries
and concerns considerably. Those feelings and emotions
combined with the conversation he needed to have with Hope
looming ahead only served to wreak havoc on his already over-
loaded nervous system.

"I'm scared to death," Drew confessed once they were
inside the truck. And he was. About becoming a father, for
sure, but also about his future with Hope as more than the
mother of his child.

"I'd like to tell you it'll get better, but that's what love does to us mere mortal men, son. It scares the living hell out of us. But I can also tell you I wouldn't trade it for anything in the world."

Neither would he, Drew realized.

And with any luck, Hope would feel the same way.

CHAPTER FIFTEEN

Tess had timed her invitation to go Christmas shopping perfectly. Since Anna had left, Hope had been strung tighter than a drum as she vacillated between calling Drew about his mother's visit, seeking solace from Sarah, or just waiting until he returned. Fortunately, Tess's call provided Hope a much-appreciated diversion.

Once Tess arrived, they drove about fifty miles south to a huge indoor mall where they combed nearly every store for the gifts needed to edge them closer to their Christmas shopping finish line. After a second trip to the car to stow their purchases, Tess suggested grabbing a late lunch. Starving, Hope readily agreed.

"I don't know about you, but I've made some serious progress on my Christmas shopping," Tess said as soon as the waitress dropped off their drinks and left with their orders.

Hope nodded. "Me too." In fact, she'd practically finished. Well, except for Drew. Funny how the person she knew best in Virginia was the hardest to shop for. Oh, she'd found some little things, mostly stocking stuffers, like a pair of work gloves, some socks, and his favorite candy. Other than that, she was kind of at a loss.

Maybe Tess would have an idea. "I'm not sure what to buy Drew, though. What do you get Jack?"

"Oh, we just do silly things. Like one time, I gave him a subscription for printer ink since he's always running out. Last year, I arranged to have his car serviced on a regular basis because he gets all involved in his writing and forgets to take care of everyday stuff like that."

"So, more practical gifts."

"Yeah. Nothing to write home about." Tess took a sip of her iced tea. "But you and Drew have a different kind of relationship than Jack and I have."

"What do you mean?" Except for Thanksgiving dinner and today, Hope had never seen Tess without Jack or vice versa.

"Well, since we spent at least forty minutes oohing and aahing over baby clothes, toys, and accessories, I'm guessing you and Drew have an intimate relationship." Tess shook her head. "Though we've known each other forever, Jack and I are just friends."

"Really?" Hope found this revelation quite interesting.

Tess furrowed her brow and gave Hope a side-eye. "Yeah, really."

"So, you two have never—"

"No," Tess interrupted, shaking her head emphatically. "Not ever. Eww."

Interesting, since Hope would have sworn there was more between them than friendship. Guess that's what happens when two people of the opposite sex have been friends since childhood.

Fortunately, the waitress arrived with their lunch before Hope could put her foot in her mouth again.

"So, back to your original question about what to get Drew for Christmas. Have the two of you never exchanged gifts before?"

"Not really. At work, everyone pitched in, and we adopted a family in need for Christmas." Though Hope had confided in

Tess about the baby, she hadn't gone into detail about all the hows and whys.

"The two of you haven't been together for any holidays until now?"

"Aside from the baby connection and a pretty intense mutual attraction, I'm not sure we're what you'd call together now." Hope dredged a fry through her puddle of ketchup. "It's a long story involving devastating news and self-medicating with a bottle of tequila to dull the pain."

"Been there. Done that. On multiple occasions."

"But without getting pregnant in the process, I assume."

"Thankfully, no." Her eyes widened. "Not that you aren't thankful or—"

"It's okay. I get it," Hope interjected. She didn't want Tess to berate herself unnecessarily. "Of course, things would be considerably less complicated if either of us had given any thought to using protection." Hope chuckled humorlessly. "I found out at an annual checkup for work. I was already through the first trimester and didn't suspect a thing."

"You had a lot going on with your father, though."

Hope nodded. "Yeah." Still do, she thought, cringing at the memory of the financial mess still awaiting her in Kentucky. "One of the biggest reasons I agreed to come home with Drew was so everywhere I looked or everyone I talked to wouldn't be a constant reminder of my dad. Not that I don't want to remember him; I just needed some time and space to work through all the emotions."

"That makes perfect sense." Tess squeezed Hope's hand. "Has being here helped?"

"In that regard, yes."

"But..."

"But when we left in November to come here, my plan was to return to Kentucky after the new year, refreshed and ready to tackle everything I left behind."

"And now?"

"Obviously, it's something I still need to do. But after being here with Drew, so much has changed."

"Like what?"

"Like...everything." Hope drew in a deep breath, exhaling slowly. "So far, we've acted and reacted but haven't actually talked in depth. At first, we did, but since being at Lone Oaks, we've just kind of decided to let things happen and see where they went."

"Are you happy about where things are between the two of you?"

"That's just it, Tess. I'm not sure where we are exactly." Sighing, Hope sat back against the cushioned booth. "Anna came to see me this morning, and we had a similar conversation. She said it was high time Drew and I talked through this. I know she's right, but what if we end up wanting different things?"

"I wish I had an answer for you, Hope, but Anna's right. The two of you need to talk this out. And chances are you will want some different things. But that's life."

"I have no idea how to even start the conversation with him."

"So many unknowns."

"Exactly."

Thoughtfully, Tess finished her iced tea. "Maybe the best place to start is to figure out what you want to happen between the two of you and go from there."

Much easier said than done, Hope feared.

By the time they returned to Lone Oaks, the temperature had dipped below freezing and snow flurries began to spiral to the ground. "How much farther do you have to go to get home?" Hope asked as she gathered her packages.

"Not far. I live on the other side of Lake Sheridan. Won't take me ten minutes to get home."

"Good," Hope replied. "Thanks so much for today, Tess. I really enjoyed myself."

"Me too. Hopefully, we can hit some of the after-holiday sales."

Hope smiled. "I'd like that."

"Good luck with your talk."

"Thanks. Be careful going home."

"Will do." Tess winked and put the SUV in drive as soon as Hope shut the passenger door.

As Tess drove off, Hope went inside. Rather than leaving her shopping bags by the door, she carried the packages to the bedroom, stowing all but one in the closet before returning to the kitchen. She set the purchase on the counter and removed her coat, securing it on one of the pegs by the door.

Thirsty, she poured herself a glass of milk and took a long sip. Then she dug into the shopping bag, pulling out half a dozen gender-neutral infant outfits, three pairs of the teensiest shoes ever, and a beautiful stuffed horse from Tess. Hope couldn't wait for Drew to see everything.

And maybe an impromptu show-and-tell of baby clothes would provide the segue necessary to begin the discussion they needed to have.

As if on cue, Drew walked in accompanied by a cool gust of air. Just the sight of him kicked Hope's pulse up several notches. But what else was new?

"Hey," he greeted her, closing the door behind him.

"Hey."

Drew unbuttoned his jacket but didn't take it off. "Did you and Tess buy out all the stores?"

"We definitely made a dent." She held up one of the sleepers. "We did find a few baby departments, and I couldn't resist."

His features softened as she held up the rest of the outfits for him to see. "Everything's so tiny."

"Considering the baby is only about the size of a coconut right now, I think everything will be plenty big enough come May."

"A coconut?"

She nodded. "On the baby app, they usually compare the size of the developing fetus to fruit or seeds. So far, he or she has grown from a poppy seed to a coconut and weighs about a pound."

"Unbelievable," Drew murmured in pure awe.

"Look at these." She handed him a pair of miniature work boots and couldn't help puddling up at how gingerly he held them in his big, strong hands. But it was the raw emotion shimmering in his beautiful blue eyes that snatched the breath right out of her lungs.

Before she could form a coherent thought, let alone try to speak, Drew set the shoes on the counter, cupped her cheek in his work-roughened palm, and lowered his lips to hers. Brief, yet quite potent, the kiss rocked Hope to her core.

Exhaling slowly, Drew rested his forehead against hers. Their breath mingled as his spicy scent combined with the fresh winter air from outside cocooned her. Aroused, Hope resisted the urge to wrap herself around Drew like a vine and beg for more of his delicious, toe-curling kisses.

But giving in to her baser instincts would only delay the inevitable and quite possibly complicate their yet-to-be-resolved situation further.

"I'm sorry you had to face my mother alone this morning," Drew apologized as if he could read her thoughts.

Smiling, Hope pulled back enough to meet his gaze. "At least we don't have to worry about how to break the news about the baby to your parents anymore."

"There is that."

Hope gestured at what she'd bought while out shopping. "Obviously, Tess also knows. She bought the horse."

"Then it's a safe bet she's already given Jack the news."

"You know, I assumed they were a couple until today when she told me they were only friends." She began to put the clothes and shoes back in the bag. "But I guess you already knew that." And what possible difference did it make when they had their own relationship to sort out?

Having this conversation shouldn't be so freaking difficult. They were two intelligent and reasonable adults who both wanted to do what was best, even if it meant stepping out of their respective comfort zones. Besides, what was worse—continuing to worry themselves into an ulcer about all the potential what-ifs or laying all their cards on the table toward finding an amicable resolution?

Best to cut straight to the chase. "Drew, we need to talk."

"I know." He swallowed visibly. "And I promise we will. But first, I have something I want to show you."

She narrowed her gaze. "What?"

Drew took her coat off the hook and handed it to her. "We need to go for a little ride to see it."

"In the snow?"

He nodded. "Dress warm."

With curiosity winning the battle over apprehension, Hope zipped herself into the jacket, yanked a knit cap on her head, and slid her hands into the leather gloves she pulled from her pocket. Drew rebuttoned his coat and grabbed a colorful granny square afghan off the back of the sofa.

"Ready?"

Hope nodded. What else could she do?

Drew took her hand and led her outside, where a beautiful palomino hitched to a sleigh awaited.

"What in the world?"

"What I want to show you is difficult to get to by vehicle and harder in the snow. A four-wheeler or snowmobile might be easier to navigate, but a sleigh ride seemed more romantic."

Hope's heart bloomed inside her chest. "I love it," she declared, her breath coming out in white puffs with each word.

Drew helped her into the sleigh before rounding the back and joining her on the red velvet bench seat. He tucked the afghan around her, then picked up the reins and gave them a gentle shake, which, along with a few clicks of his tongue, propelled the horse forward.

"Where did you get this?" Hope asked as the horse trotted through the snow under Drew's expert direction.

"My dad bought it for my mom when we were kids."

How cool. Hope snuggled closer to Drew. "So, where are you taking me?"

"You'll see," he teased with a wink. "Besides, I can't do it justice with only a description."

It took about ten minutes until they reached a vast clearing where a sparkling creek cut a wide, lazy path through the glistening carpet of white. A grove of trees stood sentinel on the far side perimeter of the stream, snow clinging to each branch as more started to lightly fall from the overcast sky.

Drew pulled on the reins, slowing the horse to a halt. Awestruck, Hope couldn't take her eyes away from the breathtaking winter wonderland stretching out in front of her. "It's absolutely gorgeous." And like the man beside her, the scene simply took her breath away.

He set the brake on the sleigh. "Even without the snow, it's still pretty impressive."

Hope turned her head to look at him. "I'm guessing it has special meaning for you." It must, or why would he have bothered to cart her all the way out here in the snow? Much less in a horse-drawn carriage in below-freezing temperatures.

Not that Hope minded. Truth be told, she'd have endured blizzard conditions to set her sights on this magnificent parcel of Lone Oaks. Especially since Drew obviously wanted her to see it.

"After Reese proposed to Olivia, my grandparents gave each of us a section of land." He inclined his head forward. "This is mine." Shifting, Drew took her hand in his and locked his beautiful eyes with hers. "I'd like it to be ours."

Hope's chest constricted on a barely audible gasp. "Oh, Drew." All other words failed her as her emotions ran amok, hitting hard and fast. Everything from shocking disbelief to abject fear to guarded happiness, each battling valiantly for supremacy over the other.

"I know it probably seems like I had this planned all along, but I didn't. In fact, when I asked you to come home with me, I had every intention of returning to Wakefield in January and accepting Neil's partnership offer. I only agreed to Pops' proposition to mollify him and spend time with my family. But only if you agreed to come with me, since there was no freaking way I could bear the thought of leaving you behind. Not for six days, let alone six weeks. And definitely not for your first Thanksgiving and Christmas without your father."

"So you've said." And he had. Repeatedly. Only this time, Hope didn't take any offense at his overprotective nature where she was concerned. How could she when it was one of the reasons she'd fallen for him so completely? "But this *is* where you belong, Drew. Returning to your roots and working with your grandfather like the two of you planned all those years ago." She smiled up at him. "It's your destiny."

"No. You're my destiny, Hope. Because without you, nothing else matters. Not where I live or where I work." Drew shook his head. "Nothing."

Though Drew's words reached right in and curled around her heart, Hope found it impossible to shake her lingering companions of doubt and apprehension. She wanted to. God, how she wanted to, but something continued to hold her back. What the hell was it?

And then it hit her.

The baby. The real reason they were together in the first place. Because if they hadn't slept together, she wouldn't have gotten pregnant, and right now, their relationship would still be strictly platonic and professional.

Right?

"What about the baby?" The question tumbled out before she could stop it. But maybe that was a good thing.

"Of course, our little coconut matters, Hope. But please believe me when I say that in no way has he or she ever defined how I feel about you." He tapped his breastbone with his fist. "Not in here. Because since the first moment I saw you, my heart belonged to you. And it always will."

Drew trailed a gloved finger along the line of her jaw. "I love you, Hope. More than I ever thought it was possible to love anyone. And though coming back and working with Pops has convinced me I don't want to limit my practice but rather expand it to include animals of all sizes and breeds, it won't mean a thing without you as my partner—professionally, but most importantly, personally."

Hope didn't think her heart could get any fuller. She was wrong. "Then I guess that means Wakefield is no longer an option."

"It doesn't rule out Louisville, though. Or even Kentucky."

"But Lone Oaks is your home."

Drew shook his head. "My home is with you, Hope. So, be it here or Louisville or even some shack in the hills somewhere in between, wherever you are is where I want to be. With you." He leaned forward and brushed a kiss across her lips. "Only you."

"And our little coconut," Hope added, tears of happiness swimming in her eyes. "I love you, Drew. And I can't think of a more perfect place than right here to build our life together."

"Are you sure? Because—"

Hope pressed her finger against Drew's lips to silence any caveats he was about to offer. "I'm positive." And she was. Gone were her doubts and concerns. Her worries and apprehension. Her fears and reservations. Every single obstacle that stood between them and this moment no longer existed.

And Hope had never been happier. "I'm glad your mother stopped by today."

"You're really thinking about my mother right now?"

With a sheepish smile, Hope nodded. "Well, yeah." She

wound her arms around Drew's neck. "She was the one who convinced me we needed to talk sooner rather than later."

His eyes widened. "So this is what you wanted to talk about back at the house?"

"Pretty much."

"Because of my mother?"

"She made a good point. Why worry about what might happen between us after the holidays when nothing was stopping us from having the discussion now and setting our minds at ease?"

Drew laughed and shook his head.

"What?"

"My father and I had a similar conversation at lunch today."

"Hence the one-horse open sleigh?"

"No." Grinning, he pulled her closer. "That was all me."

"You done good."

"Anything for you," he whispered, lowering his head toward hers.

Before his mouth reached hers, Hope pressed her palm against his chest. "There is one other thing your mother and I talked about today."

"Yeah? And what was that?"

"I invited her to be there when the baby is born."

"You did?"

Hope nodded. "She said wild horses couldn't keep her away."

"Oh, I have no doubt. Even without the invitation."

She slapped his chest playfully. "Stop."

Laughing, he curled his fingers around hers. "And God help us if our little coconut is a girl."

"Like she won't have you wrapped around her finger before the ink dries on her birth certificate."

His eyes softened. "She already does." He brought their

joined hands to the center of his chest. "And so does her mother."

Once again, tears filled her eyes. God, she loved this man.

"So, what do you say? Will you do me the honor of allowing me to make an honest woman out of you, Hope Logan?"

"I think that can definitely be arranged." Hope grinned up at him. "And the sooner the better."

A smile lit up his beautiful blue eyes, warming Hope from the inside out. "My thoughts exactly."

Hope laid her head on his shoulder, her hand over his heart —strong and steady, just like him. "Thanks for not giving up on me, Drew."

Wrapping his arm around her, Drew pressed a kiss to her forehead. "I love you too much for that to ever happen, Hope. Never doubt that."

Once again, her heart simply melted. "I love you, Drew. And I can't wait to spend the rest of my life showing you just how much."

"Me too, sweetheart," Drew said softly as he lowered his head, stopping short of her mouth. "Me too."

And when his lips met hers in a kiss that branded her soul, Hope knew she was exactly where she was supposed to be.

Home.

For now and forever.

EPILOGUE

"She's absolutely beautiful, isn't she?" Hope asked Drew as their daughter began to nurse for the first time.

"She takes after her mother," Drew answered, pressing a kiss near Hope's temple. "You did good, babe."

"I couldn't have done it without you," she replied, leaning her head against his. He'd been a champion through every second of her nearly twelve-hour labor. Never leaving her side. Making sure she was comfortable. Offering encouragement. Feeding her ice chips. Letting her squeeze his hands so tightly she feared she might have cracked a few of his metacarpals in the process.

When the baby stopped nursing and detached, Hope handed Drew his daughter and snapped her maternity bra back into place. "We should probably invite your parents in," Hope suggested. "I'm sure Anna is itching to get her hands on this little princess."

"You think?" Drew countered with a grin in his beautiful blue eyes. Ones she hoped their daughter would share. "The first girl in the family in two generations—yeah, we'll be lucky if we ever get to hold our daughter again."

"Go tell them it's okay to come in."

"Are you sure you don't want a few more minutes of peace?"

Hope rolled her eyes. "Go get your mother."

"Okay, but don't say I didn't warn you," he relented with a teasing grin as he handed their daughter back to Hope.

He wasn't gone three seconds before the door swung open, and Anna burst into the room followed a little more slowly, albeit not much, by Eli. Drew brought up the rear but quickly returned to his place by Hope's side.

Anna hovered at the edge of the bed, her eyes brimming with tears as she clasped her hands in front of her heart. "Isn't she the most precious thing you've ever seen, Eli?"

"She sure is."

"Gram, Gramps, may we present your first granddaughter, Samantha Logan Blackwood."

"Aw, you named her after your father." A tear spilled onto Anna's cheek. "I know he has to be smiling down from heaven."

Hope brushed away a tear of her own. She had a feeling Sam was beaming indeed. "Would you like to hold her?" Hope asked Anna.

"Are you sure?"

As Hope held Samantha out, Anna carefully transferred her granddaughter from Hope's arms to her own. She eased into the chair by the bed, pure devotion shining all over her face as she pressed a kiss to Samantha's forehead.

"We'll never get her back," Drew murmured as he stretched out on the bed beside Hope.

She swatted at him. "Behave."

For the next half hour, Samantha received quite the royal treatment from both her Gram and Gramps. With every minute that passed, Hope's eyes got heavier. It had been a big day, and though she didn't want to miss a minute with her daughter, she felt like she'd worked a forty-hour week doing hard labor.

Pun definitely intended.

Eli inclined his head toward Hope. "I think our new Momma needs some rest," he alerted his wife.

"Of course she does," Anna readily agreed. Rising, she reluctantly handed the baby to Drew before leaning down to press a kiss on Hope's cheek. "You need to get some sleep," Anna insisted.

"I will," Hope assured her mother-in-law. "Thanks so much for being here."

Anna squeezed Hope's hand. "I told you wild horses couldn't keep me away." She straightened and leveled one of her arched-brow looks at Drew. "You make sure she gets some rest."

"Yes, ma'am."

She leaned in and kissed Drew's cheek. "You do good work," she whispered.

"I got it. Honest," he replied with a smile he'd been wearing since the first moment he'd laid eyes on his beautiful daughter.

"Anna," Eli called from the door. "I'm sure they'll let you come back later."

Rolling her eyes, she smiled down at her granddaughter and then looked back at Hope. "It'll be all right, won't it? If we come back later, I mean."

"Like we could keep you away," Drew muttered, his eyes twinkling as he purposely yanked his mother's chain.

"Of course you can come back later," Hope assured her.

"Anna. Let's go," Eli prompted with a sweep of his hand toward the open door.

"Okay, okay." She bent to kiss Samantha's soft cheek once more and then turned to precede her husband out of the room.

"Ten dollars says she's back within the hour."

"Be grateful she wants to spend time with her granddaughter."

"Tell me how grateful you are when she moves in with us."

Hope shook her head. "You're terrible."

"But you love me anyway."

Her heart swelled inside her chest. "You're right. I do."

"I love you too. More and more each day." Cradling the baby, Drew leaned over and gave Hope a long, tender kiss. "Now, get some rest. You deserve it."

She nodded. "You can put her in the bassinet, you know."

"I will. In a little bit." As Drew held their daughter, a look of pure adoration in his beautiful blue eyes, Hope couldn't help but smile. Right there was her entire world. The child she loved more than life itself and the man she loved with every breath in her body.

Life surely couldn't get much better than that.

The End

ACKNOWLEDGMENTS

It definitely takes a village to write and publish a book, so special thanks to the following:

Jen Malone, acquiring editor for Inkubator Books, who read one of my books and liked it enough to reach out to me. And that set the publishing ball rolling. I will be forever grateful.

Inkubator Books for expanding their publishing genres to include romance and for giving me a chance to have my series included! You have made one of my lifelong dreams come true.

All my beta readers and proofreaders pre-Inkubator: Mom, Sherry, Wendy, Ann and Ashley.

The Inkubator Team for their guidance, editing, proofreading, formatting, marketing and everything that goes into preparing a book to publish and then publishing it: Garret, Brian, Jen, Claire, Alice, Ella and anyone else who has made this possible.

The Sassy Scribes (Ann, Jade, Heather, Ashley, Nico, Hana and Melanie) whose knowledge, encouragement, support, inspiration, critiques, brainstorming sessions, honesty and love have helped me become a better writer. Your selflessness to help fellow authors is unparalleled.

My sisters by heart (Sherry, Peachy, NJ, Mariah and Sara) for being the best friends a girl could ever hope to have. I couldn't do this without you believing I could do this and for constantly cheering me on.

My mom and my family: your love, support, and encouragement leave me speechless. Thank you from the bottom of my heart for everything, but most importantly for just being you!! I couldn't do it without you.

ABOUT THE AUTHOR

Isabelle Grace is a retired educator who writes sweet to steamy contemporary romance full of heart, humor, and all the feels. Each book contains swoon-worthy heroes and strong, often sassy heroines on their journey to happily-ever-after. Each story is primarily set in a small town, loosely based on her own surroundings in the foothills of West Virginia's section of the Blue Ridge Mountains.

When not writing, Isabelle loves to read and spend time with her family, friends, and her rescue Pomeranian, Bella.

———

www.isabellegracewriting.com

ALSO BY ISABELLE GRACE

Made in the USA
Middletown, DE
30 November 2023